## "DARCY ..."

The voice came again, soft . . . eerie . . . Darcy raised her head from the pillow and froze.

As the voice whispered her name, she saw a subtle darkening at the window, as if shadows had gathered just outside.

Something scratched at the screen.

Something . . . trying to get in.

In paralyzed horror, Darcy saw the outline of a hand working at the edge of the sill . . . heard the soft scraping of fingers against metal . . .

She tried to scream but couldn't.

Helplessly she saw the fingers groping across her window . . . like quick black worms squirming out of the night . . .

She scooted back against the wall, her mouth open in a soundless cry.

The fingers froze, like outstretched claws.

And as the hand pulled back into the darkness, something glittered at her and disappeared.

She saw it in that split second, a glimmer of red.

Something—*someone*—watching her with his bloodshot eye.

# VAMPIRE

## RICHIE TANKERSLEY CUSICK

**AN ARCHWAY PAPERBACK**
Published by POCKET BOOKS

New York   London   Toronto   Sydney   Tokyo   Singapore

AN ARCHWAY PAPERBACK *Original*

An Archway Paperback published by
POCKET BOOKS, a division of Simon & Schuster Inc.
1230 Avenue of the Americas, New York, NY 10020

Copyright © 1991 by Richie Tankersley Cusick

ISBN: 0-671-70956-9

First Archway Paperback printing June 1991

10  9  8  7  6  5  4  3  2  1

AN ARCHWAY PAPERBACK and colophon are registered trademarks of Simon & Schuster Inc.

Cover art by Gerber Studios

Printed in the U.S.A.

IL 7+

for
Daddy and Momma
Sassy and Fritzi

*those were good times*

VAMPIRE

# Prologue

The carnival was about ready to close.

From the doorway of her tent the old gypsy woman stood watching as a boisterous group of young people shoved its way along the path to her entry. She was tired . . . there had been so many palms and predictions taking her time today—and now she sighed wearily, counting heads as the group waved and jostled one another up to where she waited.

"One young miss . . . four young gentlemen. . . ." The gypsy woman sized them up with a practiced glance. Some special drama seemed in order for the occasion . . . her big climax to a busy day.

"Come." She motioned them in, one at a time, her eyebrows raised in speculation as each in turn was led back into the gloomy shadows and given a glimpse of the future. "And tell no one," she finished each fortune with a solemn warning, looking deep into the challenging young eyes, holding them with her older, wiser ones, "or other, unwelcome forces will surely interfere. . . ."

Each customer seemed genuinely satisfied . . . if not altogether convinced.

Except for the one she'd chosen for her grand finale.

"My poor child, I see anguish . . . despair. . . . I see terrible tragedy"—her voice lowered dramatically, her hand squeezing hard around the fingers that trembled so in her chilly grasp—"for you are not like the others. You—and you alone—walk as the Undead . . . with no choice of your fate."

If the other customers had been somewhat skeptical, this one had certainly given her the reaction she'd hoped for—the instant expression of shock and fear, the disbelief and confusion clouding the narrowed eyes.

"You understand," her client whispered. "I really believe you understand. What can I do?"

"Perhaps . . ." She thought for a long moment, staring deep into her crystal ball. "Perhaps . . . if you find your heart's true love . . . your chosen one . . ." She gave a mysterious smile. "Yes . . . your chosen one will bring you peace at last."

"Do you really think so?"

"Your chosen one. Now go. And may heaven have mercy upon you."

The gypsy woman chuckled now, watching them all leave—the reckless group of five herding one another off into the blinking neon night.

Only . . . one of them wasn't laughing anymore.

*T*he building sat back from the narrow street, dingy and cheap in the gray afternoon light. Its red neon sign blinked on and off, the words DUNGEON OF HORRORS reflecting in the puddles, turning the water to blood.

"He's insane," Mrs. Thomas mumbled, peering gloomily from the cab. "I always knew he was, but I'd hoped by now he'd outgrown it."

"How could you possibly know anything about Uncle Jake?" Darcy turned accusing eyes on her mother. "You haven't even seen him for years."

"I know what Alicia tells me, and *she* says he's a disgrace."

"Aunt Alicia thinks everyone's a disgrace."

"Darcy, I won't have you talking that way about my sister. She's a *prominent* attorney and *very* highly respected. It's no wonder Jake's a total embarrassment to her—he's *always* been a total embarrassment to both of us.''

"He can't be that bad, Mom. And I'll never understand why you and Aunt Alicia won't have anything to do with Uncle Jake, when he's your only brother.''

"I've told you before, we never *did* have anything to do with Jake. After the divorce he went to live with Father. We didn't even grow up together.'' She snorted in disgust. "He's not our kind, Darcy. He never has been, and he never will be.''

"What *is* our kind, Mom?'' Darcy said, then at the look on her mother's face, added hurriedly, "Well, I wish you weren't leaving me here. I don't like Aunt Alicia.''

"Of course you do,'' Mom said impatiently. "She's just like me.''

Darcy rolled her eyes, but Mrs. Thomas was mumbling again and didn't see.

"Believe me, Darcy, I wasn't planning on seeing Jake this time, but Alicia lives miles from town— you remember me telling you about that gorgeous country home of hers?—and I only have two hours between flights. It was more convenient for her to pick you up here on her way home from work. And quit being so difficult, will you? Think of *my* happiness for a change.''

"We always think of your happiness.'' Darcy sighed. "Mom, *please*—I don't want to stay with—''

"Oh, for heaven's sake, just wait here a minute,'' Mrs. Thomas returned sharply. "And stop complaining. Surely you can stand it with

Alicia for a little while. It's not like I'm abandoning you!"

Darcy watched helplessly as her mother got out and disappeared into the old building. For one crazy instant she actually considered making a break for freedom, but since she didn't know where to run, she took her suitcase from the cab and went inside.

"What do you mean she was called away on business? She can't do this to me!"

Darcy heard her mother's voice bordering on its familiar hysteria, and she looked curiously around the lobby as she closed the door quietly behind her. There were two other doorways—one hung with red beads which seemed to lead off into darkness, and another, closed, but not muffling the raised voices behind it.

"And it's so nice to see *you*, too," a second voice responded dryly. "After all this time, how can I be so lucky?"

"What kind of a place *is* this, anyway? And look at your *face!* What was it this time? Money again? Some crazy new deal of yours? A jealous boyfriend you had to settle up with? God, Jake, you are so *worthless!* Alicia must be out of her mind—does she really expect me to leave Darcy here with you till she gets back? Why didn't she call me?"

"She did, but you'd already left. And you're absolutely right—we both know how crazy Alicia's always been. Well, it was *great* seeing you. I'll just show you out—"

"But I don't have anyone else to leave Darcy with! And I've got to get back to the airport!"

"Gone through all your friends, huh? Down to last, desperate measures?"

"I'm on my way to Europe to get married! I can't take Darcy on my honeymoon!"

"Especially when husband—wait, what is it now? Number four? Five? Gosh, it's so hard to keep up with your and Alicia's weddings! Anyway, especially when *this* husband doesn't particularly like the idea of having a kid around—isn't that what Alicia told me? Hey, Sis, you don't have to explain anything to me. Why should I care if you want to dump her and fly off to your rendezvous?"

"Are you sure Alicia said she'd only be gone a few days?" Mrs. Thomas broke in, as if she hadn't heard a word he'd said. "Well, I suppose if it's just for a *few* days—"

"Hey, please don't consider *me* in all this. After all, *I* don't have plans—my life is *totally* at your beck and call—"

"Don't be sarcastic, Jake, that's so like you. I don't have time to argue. I have a plane to catch."

"Sure you do. Forgive me for interfering with your *busy* schedule. Where's the kid?"

"Her *name* is Darcy. She's a very sweet, lovable girl."

"Yeah? Just like her mom and Aunt Piranha, huh?"

In spite of her misery Darcy almost smiled, imagining her mother's livid expression. Walking over to a counter, she studied the brochures scattered there—WELCOME TO THE DUNGEON—and turned as the office door burst open.

"Oh, Darcy." Mrs. Thomas looked flustered. "I thought I told you to wait for me in the cab. This is your Uncle Jake. Jake, this is—for God's sake, Darcy, don't stare, it's impolite.''

Flushing, Darcy dropped her eyes, then cautiously raised them again. Even though she'd been told that Jake wasn't that much older than she, she hadn't expected such a boyish face, the thick brown hair falling stubbornly over the forehead, the faded jeans and dirty red jersey, the ratty-looking high-tops. He was tall, with a deliberate slouch, and insolent green eyes that seemed to be appraising her. One of his eyes was bruised and swollen, and there were several cuts and bruises on his tanned cheeks. He was eating popcorn from a bag, chewing slowly, one piece at a time, totally unbothered by the whole situation. *This can't be my Uncle Jake . . . this guy's gorgeous.*

"Darcy," Mrs. Thomas was saying crisply, "there's been a slight change of plans. Your Aunt Alicia had some emergency on a case she's working on, so while she's away on business, you'll be staying here with your uncle. It's only for a few days. The *minute* Alicia gets back, she'll come and get you and—"

"Drag you kicking and screaming to safety," Jake finished, returning Mrs. Thomas's glare with a sardonic smile.

Darcy hid a smile of her own as her mother handed Jake a slip of paper.

"Here's a list of hotels where we'll be staying. Not that you'll need to get in touch with me for anything." She glanced at her watch and made an irritated sound in her throat. "I've got to get back to the airport—I've got to make that connecting flight." As Jake shoved the paper into his pocket, she walked over and looked down at Darcy. "I'll try and send a postcard or something. . . . It's just that I don't know how busy we'll be. . . ."

Darcy nodded and looked away, her words squeezing painfully from her throat. "Have a nice time." She stiffened as her mother planted a kiss on her forehead.

"I love you, Darcy."

Another nod. Darcy felt her mother hesitate for a moment, waiting, and then the rush of damp air as the door closed.

The room filled with a terrible, empty silence.

"Well . . ." Jake chewed on his popcorn, slowly crumpled the bag, and tossed it at the door Mrs. Thomas had gone out. "She hasn't forgotten how to do the martyr face."

Darcy's eyes lifted, shocked, and he shrugged.

"Sorry. She *is* your dear old mom, after all—"

"No," Darcy said quickly, surprising herself. "You're right. It *is* a martyr face. I know just what you mean, only I never quite knew how to describe it."

He cocked his head at her. "Well, kid, it looks like we're stuck with each other."

Suddenly Darcy felt tears threatening. "I'm really sorry."

"For what? It wasn't your idea, was it?"

"Well . . . no . . ."

"Mine, either. Come on."

"Where are we going?"

"Don't you want to see where you'll be living?"

Darcy reached for her suitcase. "Oh, are we going to your house now?"

"This *is* my house. And my family."

8

Darcy looked confused. "Mom didn't tell me you lived here. Or that you're married—"

"I didn't *tell* her I live here. It's hardly the Ritz, if you know what I mean. And I didn't say I was married. You don't have to be married to have a family, okay?"

"I guess you're right."

"I am right. Didn't you see the sign? This is an honest to goodness Dungeon of Horrors." He paused, waiting for her to look at him again. "Think of all the mad, bad characters you've ever heard about—or read about—or shivered at in the movies. Dr. Frankenstein. The Wolfman. Dracula." He moved toward the beaded curtain and swept it aside. "They're all here. Come on. Have a look."

Hesitantly Darcy went through, stopping at once as darkness engulfed her. She felt Jake move past and saw his outline materialize ahead of her.

"Track lights in the ceiling." Jake pointed. "You'll get used to it in a few seconds."

"It's really black in here."

"Yeah, I have to keep it low like this. It's the way they like it."

"They?"

But Jake moved on ahead, and Darcy had no choice but to follow. It was almost like floating through a void, and as she groped along, cool, damp walls slid by beneath her fingertips. As they rounded a curve in the tunnel, Darcy could see a pale glow that seemed to be coming out of nowhere.

"Tableaus," Jake explained, leading her forward again. "Each character has his own little setup to really show him off. Each exhibit is set back in an alcove on its own little stage, so what you've got is a whole series of different scenes, like stills from horror movies. Here. The Mummy. Looks real, doesn't he?''

Jake stopped, pointing at a swaddled figure in the eerie light, its arms extended, dragging filthy wrappings across the floor.

''And this one.'' Jake nudged her on. ''Poor Mr. Hyde.''

Darcy peered in at the laboratory and the grotesquely transformed face of Dr. Jekyll. Before she could comment, Jake tugged her forward again.

''This one's my favorite. You *do* believe in vampires, don't you?''

As he pushed her to the guardrail, Darcy felt her skin crawl. There was the infamous Count Dracula, red lips curled back, fangs poised over the slender white neck of his female victim, who had fainted into his arms. In the very back of the alcove, practically hidden in shadows, rested a coffin with its lid raised, the red satin lining scattered with clods of earth which had spilled out onto the floor and run together in pools of shiny red blood.

Darcy turned away, strangely unsettled by the coffin. ''How many exhibits are there?''

''Twenty-five in all. But I'm adding some.''

''I never realized there were so many villains.''

In the half light Jake's smile seemed masklike. ''You'd be surprised.''

Drawing a deep breath, Darcy continued on, stopping at each scene, shuddering at all the gory details. The Wolfman in his final agonies. Frankenstein's monster ripping his restraints, lumbering up from the operating table. The hideous Creature surfacing from the swampy waters of the Black Lagoon. Jack the Ripper fleeing the gaslit alleyways of London. Witches . . . ghouls . . . murderers . . . monsters . . . the depraved and hopelessly wicked . . . Darcy saw them all, not wanting to look but compelled somehow, fascinated by the very wickedness that so repelled her. As they stood before the last exhibit, Jake moved his arms in an all-encompassing gesture.

"Like I said. My family."

Darcy shut her eyes, trying to force all the grisly scenes from her mind. "Well, at least your family's not dull."

He nodded slowly and leaned into the spotlight, the greenish glow going over his face so that his eyes and skin became one. Instinctively Darcy moved back.

"You don't want to go past here," Jake said, indicating a barricade of sawhorses at this end of the tunnel. "Those are the new exhibits we're putting together. Off-limits to the customers. Too easy for someone to get hurt. Or to hide." He cast her a sidelong glance and straightened. "Come on."

"Where are we going now?"

"To work."

"But I thought you were closed."

"Not here. At the Club." He led her back the way they'd come. "It's a few blocks from here. I manage the place, so we probably won't be seeing much of each other."

"But—I thought—" Darcy broke off as they reached the lobby. The outside door was open, and two people were trying to close it against a gust of rain.

"Jake!" A girl spun around, frizzy red hair plastered to her freckled cheeks, glasses perched on the end of her upturned nose, lips painted as red as her hair. "Wait till you hear what happened. It's not safe to go anywhere anymore."

Beside her a boy was wringing water from his wet T-shirt onto the floor. "Hey, Jake, how's it going?" As he lifted his eyes, he noticed Darcy and broke off abruptly, running one hand through his combed-back hair. His eyes crinkled up as he smiled. "Oh, sorry. Hi. You must be Darcy."

"Hi." Darcy smiled back, feeling awkward as the girl turned and held her in a long, deliberate stare. It wasn't friendly.

"Darcy"—Jake brought a towel from the office and tossed it to the bedraggled pair—"Liz . . . Kyle. Friends of mine."

"Nice to meet you." Darcy smiled again, uncomfortably. Liz was still staring, and there was an odd set to her lips that looked suspiciously like a sneer. Kyle reached out and shook Darcy's hand.

"Jake told us you were coming to visit your aunt, but I forgot it was today."

"Uhhh . . . there's been a little change in plans," Jake broke in quickly. "Looks like I have a houseguest for a while."

"Oh, great," Liz snorted, and this time her sneer was unmistakable. "Just what you love most in the world."

"So what do you think about this place?" Kyle shifted his weight slightly, as if trying to block Darcy from Liz's view. "Pretty great, huh?"

"It's . . . really fascinating." Darcy looked down at his hand still holding hers, then up again into his face. His dark hair shone with raindrops. His eyes were deep blue, with laugh lines at their corners, and there was a slight dimple in his chin.

"Just tell him," Liz said loudly. "Tell him about the murder."

"Murder?" Darcy looked alarmed, and Kyle released her hand and stepped back. His sleeveless shirt showed leanly muscled biceps, and both knees on his faded jeans were ripped out.

"Murder's nothing new," Jake said, a faint smile on his face. "Tell me something exciting, Liz."

"They found a girl in an alley over on Second Street," Liz went on. "Somebody slit her throat."

"And we knew her—sort of. She comes—came— into the Club a lot. The one always requesting songs." Kyle shook his head slowly. "She always came in alone, remember? Brandon always worried about her leaving so late all by herself—"

"Brandon doesn't think *any* girl should be by herself when *he's* around." Jake glanced slyly at Liz's furious expression and reached for Darcy's suitcase. "I'll take this upstairs. You need the bathroom or anything?"

"I'm fine," Darcy said.

"Go on and tell him the rest." Liz nudged Kyle roughly in the side. "About all the blood everywhere. And about the marks."

Kyle hesitated a moment. "Well . . . she had these marks on her neck."

"I guess she would," Jake said offhandedly, "if her throat was cut."

"No, that's not what I meant." Kyle brought one hand slowly to his own neck, frowning. "Here—right over her jugular vein—there were these marks. I mean, they didn't break the skin or anything—it was like someone painted them on."

"Like his signature." Jake shrugged. "The murderer signing his name."

"Like bite marks," Kyle said solemnly. "You know. Like . . . a vampire."

**2**

You're not what I expected," Liz said, studying Darcy with a cool stare.

Darcy moved her hands away from her ears, trying to hear through all the noise. The Club was packed, thick with smoke and dancing couples, laughter, shouting, and blaring music. From their corner booth she had a clear view of the stage where the band was finishing up its set, and as Liz spoke again, Darcy leaned closer, forcing a smile.

"What *did* you expect?"

"Someone more sophisticated, I guess. Not like a little kid who needs a babysitter for the summer. You *are* seventeen, aren't you?" Her lips moved in a mean smile. "But we hardly look the same age, you and I. In fact, Jake seems *much* older than you. I guess because he's so mature."

"Is he?" Darcy remembered Jake's jersey and

15

sneakers and all the stories her mother had told her through the years. "We're only six years apart. My mother was already twelve when Jake was born."

"He never talks about you," Liz said, as if she and Jake had had many conversations. "He never even mentions you."

"I don't guess he'd have any reason to. He and my mom aren't exactly close."

"So she dumped you." Behind her glasses, Liz's eyes looked triumphant.

Darcy met the stare and held it. "Yes. She dumped me. It's not the first time, and it probably won't be the last. As a matter of fact, I'm a *professional* dumpee."

A flicker of surprise cut across Liz's face. She reached for her glass, twirling her straw slowly. After a moment her eyes lifted again to Darcy's.

"So what do you think about him?"

"Jake?" Darcy hedged. "He's . . . not quite what I expected."

"He's wonderful." Liz's chin lifted. "And we're *very* close."

"How nice for you." Darcy forced pleasantness into her tone. "How do you know each other?"

"Kyle knew Jake first—Kyle was coming in here all the time to listen to music. And then Jake hired this band Kyle's in. I don't know how much longer that band's going to stay together. Personality problems in the group. Kyle's such an optimist, but you can bet he'll be the first one replaced—the lead singer wants all *his* buddies in the group, even though none of them are any good." She looked exasperated. "Anyway, Kyle and Jake got to be good friends, and that's how I got my job at the Dungeon. I kind of run the place. Jake spends so much time here at the Club, he doesn't really have time for that stupid horror show of his."

"Oh. I didn't know that." Darcy's eyes went to the stage, where the guys were laying down their instruments, preparing to go on break. "I love this music. Kyle's a really great drummer."

"One of the best around." Liz actually smiled. "He has great hands."

"Is he your boyfriend?"

"Boyfriend?" Liz echoed, then gave a harsh laugh. "He's my brother. Couldn't you tell?"

Darcy shook her head, flustered. "You don't look anything alike."

"You're right. He's the cute one." A smile hardened at the corners of her mouth. "But I've got the brains." For a long moment she stared at the stage, her hands twirling the glass around and around on the tabletop between them.

"That's so horrible about that murder." It was the first thing that popped into Darcy's mind, and she wished instantly that she'd thought of something else to break the awkward silence.

"Yes." Liz was looking at her again, her expression thoughtful. "Vampires. What a horrible way to die."

"But they're not real." Darcy started to laugh, then felt it stick in her throat as Liz glared at her. "I mean, you don't really believe—"

"I believe in everything," Liz said shortly. "Look, here comes the rest of the gang. Move over."

Darcy saw Kyle making his way toward their

table, with two more boys following him. Liz bent her head and spoke quickly.

"The guy with the ponytail—that's Brandon. He belongs to me." The look she gave Darcy held a silent warning. "He and Kyle are best friends. The one trailing behind is Elliott."

"Why is he wearing sunglasses in here?"

"He always wears them." Liz nudged her over even farther. "He had a motorcycle wreck last month. He's not all there, so don't be surprised at anything he does. I don't know why Kyle even bothers with him, he's so weird."

Mildly alarmed, Darcy scooted closer to Liz, making more room in the booth. As the three boys came up to the table, Brandon struck a dramatic pose and grinned down at them with a heart-melting smile.

"Congratulate me, ladies. I got the part."

"You did?" Liz's voice rose above the noise. "Oh, Brandon, I knew you would!" As Liz reached out for him, Darcy couldn't help noticing the change that came over her. Liz's coldness had totally disappeared, and the beaming smile she gave Brandon transformed her whole face until it was almost pretty. As Brandon continued to smile down at them, Darcy tried to study him without being obvious—coal-black hair pulled back in a queue, black eyes fringed with thick lashes. He could almost be sinister, Darcy thought, with his broad shoulders and dark good looks. And as she stared at him, she suddenly realized he was staring back, and she hurriedly dropped her eyes.

"Sit down," Liz ordered him. "I want to hear all the details."

"There's really not much to tell." Brandon slid easily in beside her. "I just read some lines and stuff. But I think it was my swooping that did it."

Kyle sat down beside Darcy, laughing. "Didn't you have to bite anyone?"

"Maybe that comes in rehearsals." Brandon glanced at Darcy then back to Kyle. "So where were *you?* I thought *you* were going to try out—"

"Oh, he chickened out," Liz said irritably. "As usual."

Kyle looked embarrassed. "It's not that, it's just—"

"Hey, man, I *know* you could have gotten the part—you were the only competition I was worried about." Brandon clapped Kyle on the back, but Liz gave a derisive laugh.

"He wouldn't have gotten it, Brandon, quit telling him things like that."

"I didn't have time." Kyle shrugged and did a drum roll on the table with his hands. "Anyway, I'd rather be your manager—it's a lot less work."

"He's just too *shy.*" Brandon gave him a teasing hug. "He couldn't handle all those girls swooning all over him—"

"Come on, cut it out." Kyle squirmed out of his grasp, embarrassed, and patted the seat. "Sit down, Elliott, and get me out of this."

"No," Elliott murmured.

"You're going to be so great." Liz snuggled up to Brandon's side. "I can't wait to see you in costume."

"Yeah, I'll swoop even better once I have my cape." Brandon chuckled, his eyes flicking again to Darcy. "You must be Darcy. Kyle told me you were here. I'm Brandon.'' He thrust out his arm across Liz, giving Darcy's hand a firm squeeze. ''Do you even know what we're talking about, or do you think we're completely crazy?''

Liz reached for her glass, bumping his arm away from Darcy. ''Oops. Sorry.''

For one quick instant Brandon's eyes shot to her face, his smile fading.

''Hey,'' Liz said as he stared at her, ''it was an accident. Okay?''

After a moment Brandon nodded. His voice was deep, soft, and slightly husky. ''Sure, Liz. Okay.''

''The Community Theatre Group is putting on their production of *Dracula*,'' Kyle spoke up, breaking the tension. ''And Brandon just got the lead. That's great news, man. What a choice role.''

Brandon nodded. ''Thanks. Now, you guys better show up to give me moral support.''

''Count on it. So when's the first performance?''

''How should I know? I'll be lucky to remember the first rehearsal.'' Brandon signaled the waitress and nodded to their group as she whipped out her pad. ''Cokes all around? Darcy?''

''That's fine. Thanks.''

Brandon smiled at her, and she felt an unexpected warmth inside.

''You know . . . you're very pretty.'' His eyebrows raised appreciatively, and Darcy's cheeks flamed.

Kyle chuckled. ''You're embarrassing her. Can't you behave yourself for one—''

''Her mom dumped her,'' Liz said smugly. ''Just like extra baggage.''

There was an uncomfortable silence. Darcy

looked down at her fingers twisting together in her lap.

"We really hope you have a good visit," Kyle said hastily. "There's a lot to do here in the summer—concerts, museums, art shows—there's always something going on."

"Murder," Elliott said.

Everyone turned and stared. He was standing behind Brandon, and he moved one hand slowly up to his forehead.

"It hurts," he said quietly.

Exchanging swift looks with Kyle, Brandon started to get up. "Maybe we should go," he said. "It is pretty hot in here."

"And loud," Kyle agreed. "I need to get home anyway. I can give him a ride. Liz, you coming?"

Liz looked up at Brandon. "Brandon can take me home."

Brandon cast her a sidelong glance. "Hey, sorry, but I've got some stuff I've got to do."

"Come on," Kyle said, jerking his thumb toward the door. "Unless you'd rather walk."

"Fine." Liz shoved Brandon off the end of the seat, not bothering to hide her annoyance. As Brandon stood aside to let her out, she stalked past him, throwing him a chilly smile. "Don't let stardom go to your head, Brandon. Just remember—I know what you're really like."

As Brandon looked uneasily at Kyle, Darcy felt something brush her arm and jumped as Elliott leaned in over her. His thin, pale face was framed by wispy blond hair, and she could feel the intensity of his stare behind the dark walls of his glasses.

"I'm leaving now," he said softly.

Darcy nodded, trying to avoid looking at his unsettling expression. "Goodbye, Elliott. It was very nice to meet you."

A faint smile quivered at the edges of his lips. "It was very nice to meet you," he echoed, but his voice was flat and emotionless. "It was very nice."

Again a quick look passed between Kyle and Brandon.

"Come on, Elliott." Kyle touched him lightly on the shoulder. "I'm parked close."

Elliott turned obediently, following for several steps. Then without warning he spun around, his hands gripping the edge of the table as he leaned in closer to Darcy's ear.

"I can tell the future," he whispered.

As Darcy drew back in alarm, she saw Brandon gesturing to Kyle behind Elliott's back . . . and Liz several feet away, her face hard, but curious.

"Come on, Elliott," Kyle said firmly, pulling on his friend's arm. "Let's just go."

But Elliott was bending closer, his hidden gaze traveling slowly over Darcy's face.

"I can tell the future," he said again, and his voice was chillingly matter of fact.

"Can you?" Darcy asked hesitantly.

"Yes," Elliott said. "I'm afraid you're going to die."

**3**

As Darcy stared at him, she was vaguely aware of a long, loud silence, even though the noise around her was deafening. She could see the black lenses, so close to her, and Kyle's face somewhere off to her left, and Liz approaching silently, her arms locked over her chest. It was Brandon who broke the spell at last, who pulled Elliott away and gave a choked sort of laugh.

"Come on, Elliott, we're *all* going to die—"

"So much for your psychic powers," Kyle joined in, and turned on Liz. "Did *you* put him up to this? This *sounds* like something you'd do—"

"I wouldn't give that weirdo the time of day." Liz was indignant.

"The gypsy said so," Elliott faced them solemnly. "She told me I could tell the future."

Liz rolled her eyes. "I thought we weren't supposed to tell what she said. You blew it, Elliott."

"I didn't blow it. That's not all she told me. I've always been able to tell the future. I can't say what else she told me."

"Okay, I can tell the future, too." Kyle nodded, pulling on Elliott's arm. "I see a car and a ride and Elliott feeling much better. See you later, guys." He took Elliott's elbow and guided him firmly out the door, Liz following behind.

Brandon slid in beside Darcy and offered her an apologetic smile.

"He's always been . . . different, you know? But after he had that wreck . . . well . . ." He spread his hands, his face puzzled. "I don't know. He's just Elliott. He doesn't mean anything. He just gets mixed up."

Darcy nodded slowly, rubbing the chill from her arms. "What was all that about a gypsy?"

Brandon smiled again, resting back against the seat. "The five of us went to a carnival a couple weeks ago and got our fortunes told by this old gypsy. It was just for fun—the place was closing up, and it was a spur-of-the-moment thing."

"Fortune-tellers are kind of creepy," Darcy said. "You always wonder where they come up with all that stuff they tell you."

"Well, they make it up. Nobody really believes it. But then . . . God only knows what she told Elliott. He's not like other people. We shouldn't have let him go in."

"What happened to him? In the accident, I mean."

"Head injury. He's lucky he's still alive."

"You all seem so close. Have you known each other long?"

"Since grade school. We all grew up around here . . . go to school together. Except Liz is a year ahead, so she's already out. Guess the rest of us will be graduating together next year, too . . . at least, I hope Elliott will. . . ." His voice trailed off, and he frowned down at his napkin. "Look . . . I want to apologize for the way Liz was acting."

Darcy tried to shrug it off. "It's not your fault. I just wish I knew what I've done to upset her so much."

"You haven't done anything," Brandon said quickly. "She's not the easiest person to get along with. And I should know." His laugh was humorless. "We haven't been getting along for a while now."

"That's too bad." Darcy wished she could sound more sympathetic, but Liz's insults were still too fresh.

"Well"—Brandon shrugged—"I don't like feeling smothered. But that's not your problem. Sorry."

"It's okay. She must really care about you."

Brandon said nothing. The waitress came with their order, and he suddenly grinned over at Darcy.

"We have a lot of Cokes to drink. Good thing I'm thirsty." He grouped all the glasses in the middle of the table, and they each chose one. "Guess you haven't had time to see any sights."

"Just the Dungeon of Horrors."

"Yeah, it's cool, isn't it? All those great exhibits. Now that it's summer, you'll be swamped with tourists."

"Really? It doesn't look like anybody could even find it."

"Westonport looks different in daylight. It's the oldest part of the whole city, and they've rebuilt a lot of it, tried to save all the historical stuff. There are still neighborhoods around it, though. We all live pretty close."

"Does Jake really live at the Dungeon?"

"Yeah, his apartment's upstairs. I guess he told you how he ended up with the place, huh?"

Darcy shook her head. "My mom just told me he's always been kind of eccentric."

Brandon laughed. "Eccentric. That's pretty good. Eccentric. I like it." His eyes sparkled and they swept Darcy's face. "He was really close friends with this old guy named Gus—we all knew him—he had the Dungeon for years and years—absolutely *loved* horror movies. Anyway, Gus dies and leaves everything to Jake—the Dungeon, the apartment, what money he had, and *all* his debts." He laughed again. "Jake said it'd be more trouble than it was worth, but Gus said Jake was the only one who'd take care of the place after he was gone. And Gus was right—Jake really loves that Dungeon."

"So what was Jake doing before?"

"Before Westonport? Drifting, I guess. He never talks much about his past, and some of the guys I've seen him with, I wouldn't want to meet in a dark alley, know what I mean? This club is the best thing that's ever happened here—it's a place for kids to come and have a good time without drinking or getting in trouble. Jake's tough—but he's fair."

"Is he happy?"

Brandon thought a minute. "Yeah, I guess. Who-ever knows with Jake?"

"What do you mean?"

"He's such a loner. Jake only lets you know what he wants you to know." Brandon nodded to himself. "So what's the situation between him and your mom?"

"There *is* no situation." Darcy gave a short laugh. "She was older when he was born, so they pretty much led separate lives. From what I hear, he was pretty unconventional, and she was pretty intolerant."

"So your mom's never in touch with him?"

"Only when she wants something. Like when Gran and Gramps died, and Mom fought the will. And when my father died, and she needed money."

"Wow." Brandon's eyes widened. "She came to Jake for *money?*"

Darcy nodded, looking puzzled. "Yes, and he even gave her some. So all these years I thought Uncle Jake was very rich."

Brandon threw back his head and hooted with laughter, making Darcy smile.

"Now that I've seen the Dungeon, I guess I had the wrong picture of him." She laughed along.

"You sure did." Brandon gasped for breath. "Wow . . . Jake gave your mom money. Yeah . . . Jake's all right. But he's not rich."

"He shouldn't have given her anything," Darcy said seriously. "Not after the way she's talked about him and ignored him. If I were him, I wouldn't have given her a penny. Oh, well . . ." Her voice faded, and she leaned her elbows on the table. "She won't have to worry about money now. *This* husband comes with all the trimmings."

Brandon watched her, his face softening. "So . . . how long are you staying?"

They hadn't heard Jake approaching, and now he nudged Brandon over.

"I hear you got the part." Jake nodded approvingly. "Didn't I tell you not to worry?"

"Well, I *was* worried." Brandon looked sheepish. "Trying out in front of everyone like that—I was scared to death."

"You were not. You loved it." Jake looked as if he doubted Brandon's sanity. "Look at him," he ordered Darcy, "the hair, the eyes, the voice—he's a natural, I told him that. All that's missing are the teeth."

"I tried to get *this* guy to audition, too." Brandon nudged Jake, who looked at them askance. "I mean, he knows so much about vampires."

"Knowing and being are two *very* different things," Jake said. "There's having the knowledge . . . and having the heart."

Brandon chuckled. "Jake thinks there *are* still vampires in the world."

"There are." Jake sat straight, his eyes going from one to the other. "It's not just a myth. It's a whole race of beings. They've been around since time began. They're here with us now."

Brandon rolled his eyes. "Where? In this club?"

"Here. In this universe. And where you least expect them." Jake shrugged as if discussing the weather.

"Right. Drinking people's blood and sleeping in coffins." Brandon took a long swallow of Coke.

"Dancing out there, even as we speak. Dead people."

"Not dead. Undead."

"Same thing."

"No. It's worse than being dead. It's being trapped in some hideous twilight state *between* life and death. Doomed to live forever with no hope—ever—of dying. Of finding peace." Jake leaned slowly forward, taking Brandon's collar, pulling him closer until their faces practically touched. "If you're going to be a vampire," he said quietly, "then you'd better understand how they think."

As Darcy stared at them, she saw Brandon's head nod, a strange, trancelike movement, and Jake eased himself back into the shadows against the wall.

"Can we talk about something else?" She shivered. "Something normal?"

"Why don't you take Darcy home?" Jake stood up and handed Brandon a key. "She can use this one to go in and out. I'll be home late, Darcy, so don't wait up. Your room's on the third floor—the attic."

As he walked away, Darcy turned anxious eyes on Brandon. "But I thought you told Liz you had something to do."

"Yeah." Brandon smiled, offering his hand to help her up. "Take you home."

The rain had slowed to a fine drizzle, blurring the streets into ominous gray shadows. As Brandon kept ahold of her hand, they passed bars and cafés and narrow alleys leading off into nothingness. The sidewalks were practically deserted, and heat hung in the air like a thick fog.

Darcy heard a noise behind them and glanced back, seeing nothing. "Are we close yet?" she asked nervously. Brandon didn't seem to have heard anything. He looked down at her, pointing vaguely with his free hand.

"About three more blocks. Don't you remember the way we came?"

"I'm terrible at directions. I get lost in my own backyard."

"Hmmm . . . so I could take you anywhere, and you wouldn't even know." Brandon grinned and pulled her closer. "Sorry I don't have an umbrella."

"I don't mind. It's really not that bad."

"It's kind of quiet tonight, but on Fridays and Saturdays the crowds are unbelievable."

"I wish some of the crowds were around now." Darcy tried to laugh. "It's kind of scary."

Brandon glanced around, nodding. "Yeah, I guess. If you're not used to it."

"It's just that Liz and Kyle were talking about some murder," Darcy said. "Somewhere around Second Street?"

"Yeah, that's on the other side of town. Their cousin Tony's a cop." Brandon chuckled. "They're always finding out stuff the general public's not supposed to know." He squeezed her hand and winked. "Don't worry. You're with Count Dracula, remember? Nobody in their right mind would attack Count Dracula."

"But Kyle said there were marks on the girl's neck," Darcy insisted. "Like vampire bites."

Brandon slowed a little, guiding her around a

break in the sidewalk. "Yeah, he told me, too, but I'm not sure you really want to hear about it. It's not the best kind of bedtime story."

"Why not?"

The look he gave her was amused. "Oh, I get it. You *want* to know, but you *don't* want to know."

In spite of herself, Darcy laughed. "I guess that's right."

"Don't you have crime where you're from?" he teased. "Don't people ever get murdered?"

"This just sounded so . . ." Darcy thought back, hearing Liz's vivid description all over again. "Gruesome," she finished.

Brandon's expression was hidden in shadows. "It *is* pretty gruesome," he agreed. "There've been murders before, but nothing like this. Whoever did this had to be *really* crazy."

"Do the police have any clues?" Darcy asked.

"Not really. And you can be sure they'll try to keep it quiet. This is a tourist town. They can't afford bad publicity."

Darcy shuddered in spite of the warm night. "What kind of a person would do something so horrible?"

"Yeah, it's weird, isn't it?" Brandon paused a minute, thinking. "Like those marks not breaking the skin. They're just these two red dots, made with lipstick."

"Lipstick?"

Brandon nodded. "Like someone just pressed it real hard against her neck, then bore down and twisted it. Like trying to put in a screw or something. And it's *deep* red. Tony saw it himself. Deep, deep red."

"So they're supposed to look like bites?" Darcy wondered aloud. "Like someone—or something—*bit* that girl on the neck?"

"We're here." Brandon paused outside the lobby door and fished in his pocket for the key. "You know . . . you're taking this whole thing awfully well."

"The murder?" Darcy glanced at him in surprise, then saw his sympathetic expression. "Oh," she said, half smiling. "You mean my situation."

"Sorry," he mumbled. "It's none of my business."

She placed one hand lightly on his arm and peered up into his face. "It's happened so many times, Brandon. It's always so hard at first—especially when it's family I don't know, or even some of Mom's friends I'm not crazy about. I just have to try and make the best of it." She thought a moment. "At least, this time it's someone intriguing. I mean, I always wanted to meet my Uncle Jake, and here I am."

"Yeah." Brandon smiled. "Here you are." He held her eyes for a moment, then cleared his throat and led the way inside, taking her up a flight of steps hidden behind a door in the rear of Jake's office. "Well, this is it." He ushered her into the living room, shaking his head. "Maybe having you around will help his sense of style."

"Are you kidding—I wouldn't change a thing," Darcy joked, eyeing the clutter, the shabby furniture, the half-eaten food on the end table. "It's so . . ."

"Jake," Brandon finished with a grin. He hurried around turning on lights, then bounded up another flight of steps, reappearing again as quickly as he'd gone. "Everything looks okay. Nobody hiding in the closets. Oh, I almost forgot—" He picked his way across the messy floor and scribbled on a notepad that lay atop the TV. "My phone number. Just in case."

"In case what?"

"Well"—he shrugged—"you never know. In case anything."

"Thanks. And thanks for bringing me home."

"My pleasure. Will you be okay now? Need anything?"

"Trust me. Solitude is one of the things I handle best." She stood watching as he went back down the stairwell and hoped she sounded casual. "So . . . I guess . . . I'll see you around."

He stopped, deep in thought, then looked up at her with a mysterious smile. "There's no telling *where* you might see me. Vampires can take the shape of anything they want. Good night."

Darcy locked the door behind him, surveying the comfortable disorder with a sigh. *At least I can clean the place up while I'm here and earn my keep.* She straightened up as best she could, and then with the help of a kitchen broom and an old towel she got the place swept and dusted. Rubbing her empty stomach, she wandered into the kitchen, poured herself some milk, and scrounged three stale cookies from a nearly bare pantry. *Grocery store,* she made a mental note. *Healthy food. Cleaning supplies. Trash bags.*

She found her room with no trouble and smiled at the hasty effort Jake had put into making her feel welcome. The room still smelled musty from disuse, though its one small window was raised to the damp night air. The ceiling sloped down on all sides, making it little more than a cubbyhole beneath the eaves, but there were clean towels on the foot of the bed and red carnations in a jar on the table by the bed. *Dresser . . . chair . . . hmmm . . . no mirror. . . .*

Yawning, Darcy set her snack on the dresser and started toward the bed, yet as she reached for the covers, her hand stopped in midair. It hadn't been obvious when she'd first walked in, but now she could see the bedspread crumpled in one spot near her pillow, a faint impression still visible. *Like someone was sitting there.* . . . Darcy lifted the covers and stared at the bed. Even the pillow didn't look quite right, somehow, tilted at one end and off center, not flat and even upon the sheets as it should have been. . . .

Frowning, she glanced around the room, an uneasy chill creeping along her spine. And then . . . slowly . . . she began to raise one edge of the pillowcase.

She saw the tail first.

Against the stark white sheets it looked like a long worm, thick and grotesque—and as Darcy stared in horror, the furry body came into view, stretched out so neat and stiff in her bed . . .

She screamed then, flinging the pillow, stumbling back against the door, trying to get away from the huge, brown dead thing.

She thought it was a rat . . .

But there was only a bloody hole where its head should have been.

arcy!"

The shout came from downstairs, and a second later Jake burst into the room, his face ashen.

"What is it? Are you all right?"

Unable to speak, Darcy pointed toward the bed and watched as Jake cautiously approached.

"Holy—" He broke off, shaking his head in disgust, pulling a crumpled handkerchief from his back pocket. "That's okay—I'll get rid of it."

"Okay?" Darcy regarded him in dismay. "That's the most horrible thing I've ever seen! I was just getting the bed ready and—" She broke off, not trusting herself to speak, and Jake picked the rat up by its tail.

"Did I tell you I have cats? Strays, I mean. They come and go all the time. I must have left the door open."

Darcy kept staring at him. "A cat? You think a cat did this?"

Jake faced her, the headless rodent dangling from his handkerchief. Darcy fought off a wave of nausea and clamped her arms around her chest.

"Well, what *else* could it have been," Jake said smoothly, "if not a cat?"

Darcy looked back to the bed. "So one of your cats moved my pillow, hid that thing under there, put the pillow back on top, and spread up the bed again. You must have very talented pets."

"Look." Jake pointed to the rumpled bedspread. "See this? This means one of them—Lester, probably—made a little nest for himself. My guess is, he worked his way up under the covers from the floor, hid the rat, then laid down to guard it."

"So where is he now?"

Jake shrugged. "Out the way he came in. What's the big deal? It's easy for a cat to slip in with the customers, and none of the basement windows close all the way."

Darcy nodded slowly, her glance going back to the bed. The very thought of touching it made her skin crawl.

"I . . . don't mean to be a bother," she said, and Jake looked uncomfortable. "It just . . . really scared me."

"Yeah, well . . ." Jake sighed, shifting the rat to his other hand. "Let me get rid of this thing, and then I'll find you some more sheets. When I walked in and heard you scream, it didn't do *my* heart any good, either, let me tell you."

In spite of herself Darcy smiled. "I thought you'd be late."

"I had to get something." Jake slipped out the door. "I'll be back in a minute."

Darcy realized she was still shaking. She stripped the sheets, then opened her suitcase and started putting her clothes away just as Jake returned with a blanket.

"Sorry." He dumped it on the chair. "I don't have anything clean. I'll go to the laundry tomorrow."

"Don't worry, I can go," Darcy assured him.

"Whatever. This is probably too hot, but at least it's something."

"I'll be fine. Thanks."

"Well . . ." He stepped back, his quick glance going over the room. "I've got to get back to the Club. I can't stay with you."

"I don't want you to," Darcy said simply. "I don't mind being alone."

"You're *not* alone."

Darcy looked startled. "But . . . you said . . ."

*"They're* downstairs." Jake paused in the doorway. "You know. My family."

As Darcy watched the door close and heard Jake's footsteps fading down the stairs, her bravado began to fail her. She went to the window and looked down into the darkness, fighting back angry tears. She thought of her mother, off on a European honeymoon with a new husband Darcy hardly knew . . . of Uncle Jake's indifference to the rat in her bed . . . of Liz's deliberate snubbing. She thought of the exhibits downstairs, the twisted faces and twisted minds lurking just two floors below. *Come on, Darcy, you're a big girl. . . . You're just lucky Jake's being as nice to you as he is. . . . After all, he didn't ask for you, and he doesn't know what to do with you—so what if he's a little strange? At least he's not a total phony like Mom, at least he's interesting, at least—*

She looked back at her bed and shivered. *How could a cat have done that?*

But she *wanted* to believe Jake's story, because why else would a rat be there in her bed, like a sinister omen . . . like a hideous warning. . . .

She stared hard into the night shadows, then reached out and slowly lowered the window.

**5**

The girl hesitated at the entrance to the alleyway.

She hadn't meant to stay so long after work, and now she was sure to miss her bus. Up and down the block darkened windows stared back at her from closed shops, and she gave an uneasy shudder. She'd take the shortcut after all.

Halfway down the alley she suddenly stopped. Something was blocking the path in front of her.

Through the gray mist it seemed strangely like a shadow, hazy and still.

The girl glanced nervously over her shoulder into wet, empty blackness.

The shadow didn't move.

With her heart hammering she squared her shoulders and started walking again, keeping her eyes straight ahead.

"You must choose," a voice said in her ear. "It must be your choice."

The girl gasped and jumped back. *My God, I didn't hear him coming, didn't see him move, how did he get so close so fast.* . . . She felt the smoothness of satin brush against her arm as he towered over her. She heard the soft rustle of material and saw the long, black cape swirling around his feet.

Staring, she tried to see his face, but his head was bent and his eyes were hidden.

"Look," she said, but her voice trembled and she knew he heard her fear. "I'm meeting someone. That's probably him now."

She raised a hand, pretending to wave, and felt fingers clamp onto her arm.

"Will you stay with me?" the voice said quietly.

And again she stared . . . again his eyes were hidden.

"Look, you," she raised her voice, "get away from me right—"

"Will you?" And the eyes, at last, began to raise . . . the voice so soft . . . so persuasive. . . . "Will you—"

"Get out of here, you creep!"

Angry now, she flung off his arm and turned to run.

She never took a step.

He caught her so suddenly that she didn't even fight him, his arm beneath her chin, forcing back her head, his voice, his soft, calm breath trailing down her neck . . . lingering in her ear . . . whispering. . . .

"Will you stay with me in eternity?"

And horror flashed in her eyes then, as she realized—*finally*—what was happening . . . the cold, steel blade against her throat—the swift, searing pain—

And in the last second of her life she tried to scream.

**6**

*I* can't find anything."

As Darcy came into the kitchen, Jake got up from the table and scowled at her.

"You cleaned up the place. I can't find a damn thing."

Darcy was taken aback. "I'm sorry. It's just that . . . I thought . . . I was trying to help." She waited for an apology, but he only fiddled with the coffeemaker. "Don't you think it looks better?" she coaxed him.

"You want cereal? Toast? Both?"

"Neither. I'm not awake enough yet. I kept having nightmares all night. Rats and things."

"Yeah, okay." Jake poured a cup of coffee and slid it down the counter toward her.

"Wow. Not a spill." Darcy looked impressed.

"From my short-order cook days. Among other things."

"What other things?"

"Butcher. Baker. Garbage Taker. Only now I'd be called a Sanitation Engineer, I think."

Darcy sank into the chair and rested her elbows on the table, chin in hands. "I didn't hear you come in last night."

"I never get in early. Early night, that is."

"Doesn't the Club ever close?"

"That doesn't mean the boss quits working."

"Oh." Darcy spooned some sugar into her cup and stirred it thoughtfully. "I was wondering . . . how come there aren't any mirrors around here? Not even in the bathroom. . . ."

Jake busied himself at the counter and didn't look at her. "Mirrors?" He was silent for a long moment, then glanced back over his shoulder. "Gus was pretty blind the last years of his life. He didn't need mirrors. When I got this place, I just never got around to buying any." He picked up his own coffee mug and sat down opposite her. "Ready to work?"

Darcy looked surprised. "What am I doing?"

"Earning minimum wage. You're in charge of the Dungeon."

"I am? How do I do that?"

"Stand in the lobby and welcome people. Take their money. Hand them a brochure. Tell them to have a good time."

"I thought Liz did all that," Darcy mumbled.

"Liz is too sour. She scares people away. As a matter of fact, *she* should be one of the exhibits." He stood up and stretched. "Anyway, I fired her."

43

"You *what?*"

"Fired her. Last night when she was leaving the Club. I told her I was giving you the job instead."

"Why did you do that?"

"Oh, I've been wanting to for a long time. You were a good excuse."

"Oh, God . . ." Darcy covered her face with her hands. "Thanks a lot. As if she doesn't hate me enough already—"

"Forget it." Jake headed for the door. "She hates everyone."

Darcy followed him glumly downstairs to the office as Jake kept talking.

"You'll be working with Elliott. You met him last night, right?"

Darcy felt her stomach sink. "The guy who had the wreck? *He* works here?"

"Sure. Who else would fit in so well?" Jake started for the Dungeon, motioning her to follow. "He's my security. Makes sure no one steals anything from the exhibits."

"He doesn't look very strong to me. How could he stop anyone from stealing?" Darcy followed Jake through the dark tunnels, noticing how he acknowledged each mannequin by name, as if every one of them was an old friend being met on the street. She rubbed the goose bumps from her arms and tried not to look at the monsters as she went by.

"He hides," Jake said, picking up the conversation again. "Elliott's very good at hiding."

"Will I . . . you know . . . have to come in here?" Darcy asked.

Jake glanced back over his shoulder. "You really don't like my family much, do you?"

They stopped, and Darcy found herself looking up into the pitiless eyes of Count Dracula as he anticipated the taste of his victim.

"He's so perfect." Jake lifted an eyebrow. "Don't you think?"

Darcy's eyes fastened on the Count, who looked back at her with a fixed, shiny gaze. "He looks pretty real," she admitted reluctantly.

Jake reached out and rearranged the hem of the cape ever so slightly. "Brandon has the look," he said quietly. "He's a natural."

Darcy felt the hair prickle along the back of her neck. As she reached up to rub the chill away, she suddenly touched skin that wasn't her own—long fingers brushing against her shoulders. With a scream she jerked back and saw Elliott's ghostly face hovering beside her.

"You're so cold," Elliott said softly. "When I touch you . . . you feel like death."

"Don't sneak up on me like that!" Darcy's voice came out harsher than she meant it to, and she struggled for control. "You scared me to death, Elliott. Please don't ever do that again."

He nodded slowly, as if trying to capture every word, every gesture in his brain. "I'm very quiet when I move," he said at last.

Darcy took another step away from him, and Jake tapped her shoulder.

"Okay, I'm going to leave—if you need anything, help yourself. And if you don't see it, ask Elliott. And if Elliott can't help you, call the Club. The number's by the phone." He walked around her and peered urgently into Elliott's face. "Got that, Elliott? You'll help Darcy out here, right? Great."

As Jake went back through the tunnel, Darcy hurried to catch up with him.

"Wait—where should I do the laundry?"

Jake turned with a blank look. "You've only been here one day. How dirty can you get?"

"The sheets," Darcy reminded him as they reentered the lobby.

"Oh, yeah. That." He waved one arm vaguely. "Up the street. About five blocks or so." And with that he was gone, leaving Darcy staring at the front door.

"What do you want me to do?"

Darcy whirled as Elliott spoke behind her. She didn't have to see his eyes to feel the creeping intensity of his stare.

"Look, Elliott, I'm not your boss, okay? We're just working together. Just do what you always do."

He nodded. Then very slowly he turned and went back into the Dungeon.

Darcy busied herself arranging souvenir postcards on the counter, relieved when ten o'clock brought some curious sightseers. She gave them a cheery welcome and a brochure, then sat back, amused, as their nervous laughter and screams drifted back from the tunnels. She wondered where Elliott was hiding and hoped he wouldn't step out unexpectedly and give someone a heart attack.

At noon she suddenly remembered how long it had been since she'd eaten and went to ask Elliott about lunch. She couldn't find him in the tunnels, and when she called, only silence answered. Puzzled, she made the rounds of all the exhibits. If Elliott was trying to play a joke on her, it was certainly working—she seemed to be the only living person in the whole Dungeon.

"Elliott?" She tried to sound authoritative, but her heart was beating wildly. "Come on, Elliott, this isn't funny. Stop playing around, and let's get some lunch."

No answer. Darcy glanced nervously to her left and saw Dr. Frankenstein's laboratory . . . the sickly greenish light . . . the tray of surgical instruments, all neat and gleaming in a row. The monster's contorted face looked straight at her.

"Elliott?" Darcy yelled, but it sounded almost pleading. She forced her eyes to the darkness ahead, then froze as a soft creaking sound echoed down the tunnel. "Elliott," she whispered, "is that you?"

"Yes," he murmured. "It's me."

His hands slid over her shoulders, and Darcy whirled around, looking fearfully at his pale face.

"Where—where *were* you?" Stammering, she twisted out of his grasp, and she could feel them, his eyes, following her from behind the dark glasses.

"You should know this," Elliott said. "I think another body will be found tonight."

# 7

"What do you mean?" Darcy tried to breathe again, tried to calm her racing heart.

Elliott turned and began walking away.

"Wait! Where are you going?"

He stopped and looked back at her. "Don't you want to eat? I got some lunch."

"You did? When?" Still shaking, Darcy went back to the lobby, where Elliott was arranging slices of pizza across the counter.

"I hope you like vegetarian. That's what I got . . . vegetarian."

Darcy hardly glanced at the topping. "It's fine. Now, what about this body?"

He kept realigning the pizza, making new patterns. "Well . . . I think it might have happened again."

"What did? Another murder?"

He nodded. "The throat. Just like the other one. The police are calling him the Vampire, you know. Because so much blood's drained out. And because of the marks on the neck. They're not real bites," Elliott mused, "but they're supposed to be. They're right over the jugular." His hand slid slowly along the left side of his neck. "And that's where vampires bite, you know." His face was leveled at hers. "The jugular vein."

Darcy looked down at the untasted pizza. "What about this new murder, Elliott?"

"It happened in my dream last night. So maybe it's happened again."

"Where?" Darcy's eyes searched his expressionless face. "Where will this murder happen?"

He shrugged and turned away. "We have customers," he said.

Hurriedly Darcy swept everything off the counter and into a bag just as a noisy group came through the door. It was just the beginning of a constant stream of visitors—by the time the lobby finally cleared and Darcy had a chance to grab a bite of cold pizza, it was after five. She hadn't seen Elliott all afternoon and was just debating whether or not to look for him when he suddenly materialized through the beaded curtain, startling her.

"Elliott, I wish you'd quit sneaking around like that!" she said crossly. "What time do we close up?"

"I wasn't sneaking." Elliott stared at her.

"Well . . . do you know what time we close?"

"Now. We can lock the doors now."

Darcy nodded and came around the counter. "Okay, you go on, and I'll lock up after you."

"I have a key." He reached into his jeans pocket and withdrew the key, letting it dangle, swinging it ever so slightly. "I have my very own way to get in, as you can see."

Darcy looked back at him, trying to appear calm. "Then I have some things to do. Should we check out this place before we leave or anything?"

"I do that. That's my job."

"Okay, then." She backed toward the office, not liking the idea of leaving him there, thankful that the apartment door had a lock on the other side. "I guess I'll see you tomorrow." She couldn't tell from the slight movement of his head if he'd nodded or not. She turned and hurried upstairs.

After gathering up some dirty towels from the bathroom and kitchen, Darcy bundled everything up with the sheets and let herself out through the lobby. The weather was still muggy, the sun weakening behind a late blanket of clouds. She found the self-service laundry with no trouble and threw in a load, then went back outside. This would be a perfect time to do some exploring, and there was so much in Westonport to see. She covered every block, checking out every shop window and posted menu, then stopped in front of a quaint brick building to read its old-fashioned sign.

WESTONPORT PLAYHOUSE
COMING SOON:
*DRACULA*

She hadn't really intended to go in. But as she inched her way into the small lobby and through some doors, she saw a stage at the front and recognized Brandon's voice.

"It's my hour," he said softly. "The hour of darkness."

"Again," the director urged from a front-row seat. "Put more *feeling* into it."

"It's my hour—"

"More *menace*, Brandon, more *danger!* It's the last thing she hears before you sink your teeth into her!"

Darcy craned her head, trying to see Brandon's face as he embraced a girl onstage.

"It's my hour . . ." Brandon began, his voice hardening. "My . . . hour—"

"Sorry, but you're not supposed to be in here," someone said quietly behind her.

As Darcy turned around, a relieved smile went over her face.

"Kyle—it's me."

"Darcy!" The boy looked surprised and then pleased. "What are you doing here?"

"It was just an accident." She tried to keep her voice down, noting some annoyed stares from the stage. "I was just out sightseeing—I didn't even know the theater was around here. I know I shouldn't have come in—"

"Hey, forget it. Come on and sit down. Rehearsal's almost over for tonight—I just stopped by to make sure Brandon didn't back out." Laughing, he steered her down the aisle, and they hurriedly took some seats. "He's good, don't you think?"

"I think he'll be wonderful," Darcy agreed. "Does he want to be an actor?"

Kyle nodded, looking amused. "It's a toss-up

with music. But I tell him, hey, do both. He'll make it in whatever he chooses. He's really dedicated.''

"Well, that's a big part of the challenge."

"But I mean *really* dedicated. Like when he wants to learn a new song or something, he'll spend hours—days—until he's got it down perfect. I mean, he won't think of *anything* else. He saturates himself. He becomes that music."

Darcy listened with interest, but half her attention kept wandering back to the stage . . . Brandon's voice . . . Brandon's graceful movements across the floor. . . .

"And like this play," Kyle went on. "This Dracula guy. Brandon really wanted this part. So he's been going nuts over vampire stuff—you know, reading books, watching movies, taking notes. Trust me, from here on out he'll be eating, sleeping, breathing vampires."

Darcy thought back, remembering Brandon and Jake's conversation last night . . . *"If you're going to be a vampire, then you'd better understand how they think. . . ."*

"What is it about vampires"—she gave an involuntary shudder—"that makes them so . . . so dangerous . . . yet so fascinating at the same time?"

Kyle stared at the players onstage . . . at Brandon bowing low over his intended victim. "I never knew that much about vampires . . . but Brandon's getting to be a real authority. They're just make-believe. I don't understand getting that much into something that's not real." He shrugged apologetically.

"What do you like getting into?" Darcy asked,

loving the way his eyes crinkled up when he smiled.

"My bike. Going ninety miles an hour out on the road when there's nobody around."

"Kyle," she scolded, "don't you know how dangerous that is? You could kill yourself!"

The grin widened. "Come on, Darcy, there're easier ways to die."

They hadn't heard Brandon approaching, but now he plopped into the seat in front of them, furrowing his brow, making his voice low and deep.

"Then allow me to help you, my friend," he hissed. "I can show you how *verrrry* easy it is to die."

"That's terrible." Kyle drew back. "What kind of an accent is *that?*"

Brandon faked a hurt look. "My best Transylvanian—don't you like it? And how did you get in here anyway? Rehearsals are closed to the general public."

"I just told them I was your coach." Kyle grinned. "And that I was here to make sure you got lots—and *lots*—of practice."

"He *is* my coach." Brandon nodded at Darcy. "A coach and a traitor. We practiced lines together, and then he abandoned me. I'm starved." He smiled, leaning forward. "Hi, Darcy, how about a bite?" He flung an arm around her shoulder and pulled her close, baring his teeth. "Right . . . about here."

With a little squeal Darcy jerked away while Kyle and Brandon started laughing.

"Mmmm . . . a ticklish neck." Brandon winked. "I'll have to remember that."

"Well, then, as *usual,* I guess it's up to me to protect the girl." Kyle stood up, pulling Darcy to her feet.

"Yeah?" Brandon followed them out into the lobby. "And who's going to protect the girl from *you?*"

Squeezing Darcy between them, they headed down the street, arguing about dinner, finally deciding on a sidewalk café. Brandon and Kyle spent the whole meal trying to top each other's jokes, and Darcy could hardly eat for laughing so hard. As she finally finished, she leaned back in her chair, watching the sun sink behind the rooftops, closing her eyes lazily, then opening them again. On either side of her Brandon and Kyle were involved in another animated discussion, and neither noticed at first as she stiffened and rose halfway from her chair.

"Hey, you leaving?" Kyle was the first to reach out for her arm, forcing her back into her seat.

"It's Elliott." Darcy tried to get up again, her gaze going back and forth over the passers-by on the sidewalk and the street beyond.

"Elliott?" Brandon leaned forward, his smile fading a little at the look on her face.

"Yes. I saw him. Right over there." Darcy got up again, pointing. "I'm sure it was him."

"It couldn't have been." Kyle reached over, stealing a french fry from Brandon's plate. "He's at work now."

"Work? But I thought—"

"Oh, that's just his day job at the Dungeon,"

Kyle explained. "He works nights part-time at a gas station over on Second Street."

Darcy turned back around, conscious of their eyes on her. "Well, it had to be him. His face is— I mean—" She stopped, flustered.

"Unique?" Kyle finished helpfully.

Brandon nodded. "Yeah. That's kind of you. Unique."

"I only meant," Darcy started defensively, then realized they were teasing her. "Well, it *looked* like him."

"Where was he?" Kyle asked.

"Right over there in that alley," Darcy pointed. "He was just standing there like he was staring."

"At us?" Kyle stood up, squinting. "Was he staring at *us*?"

"It couldn't have been Elliott." Brandon slapped Kyle's hand as it casually reached for another fry.

"I guess not," Darcy said uneasily. "But it sure looked like him."

"Yeah, are you two getting along okay?" Kyle scooted back, stretching out his long legs.

"I really don't see much of him," Darcy said. "He mostly stays back in the Dungeon."

"Yeah, Elliott likes the dark." Brandon nodded, then placed one finger above his cheek. "It's his eyes. They're really sensitive to any kind of light, so he tries to stay out of it as much as he can."

"Can he really tell the future?" Darcy burst out.

Brandon and Kyle stared at her, then at each other.

"Are you serious?" Brandon shook his head, a smile playing over his mouth.

"He told me today that someone else might have been murdered."

For a moment there was silence, and then Brandon groaned softly.

"Well, there's bound to be *someone* who's been murdered lately *somewhere* in the universe."

"No, he was serious. He meant the Vampire. That's what he told me."

"Elliott lives in a fantasy world," Kyle said, not unkindly. "He likes to make things up. He still swears a UFO hit his bike and caused his wreck."

Kyle looked so solemn saying it that Darcy stared at him, her eyes narrowed.

"You're joking."

"He's not." Brandon shook his head, smiling sadly. "I swear he's not. Poor Elliott." He looked at Kyle, then at Darcy, and without warning the three of them erupted into laughter.

"You guys, that's not *funny!*" Darcy protested, wiping her eyes on her sleeve.

"I know it's not." Kyle sank back in his chair, holding his stomach. "But, God, I mean . . ." His voice trailed off as he glanced at his watch, then bolted upright. "Man, I've got to run! I didn't know it was so late!"

Brandon checked his own watch and got up. "Me, too. It's not smart to be late for rehearsals. What are your plans, Darcy?"

"My laundry," Darcy remembered. "I just hope no one's stolen it by now."

"Wow." Kyle whistled. "You mean Jake's got you doing his dirty work already?"

"Not exactly." Darcy made a face as they headed out onto the street. "His cat left a present for me in my bed last night. A dead rat." She saw their disgusted faces, then added, "Without its head."

Brandon gave an exaggerated shudder and looked over at Kyle. "But I thought Jake didn't have his cat anymore."

"He doesn't," Kyle answered. "It died last spring sometime."

Darcy slowed down, frowning. "But that can't be. He said his cat did it. He called it by name . . . Lester, I think."

"Yeah, that's right, Lester." Brandon nodded, shoving his hands in his pockets. "He was always carrying in dead stuff, I remember that. But Lester died."

"Wait a minute," Darcy insisted. "Then if Lester's dead—"

"Relax." Brandon patted her shoulder. "Jake's always taking in strays, and he probably started calling one of them Lester."

"That sounds like Jake." Kyle grinned. "Rather than go to all the trouble of thinking up a brand-new name. Well, here's where I leave you. See you guys later."

"Right." Brandon gave a wave, then steered Darcy over to the opposite corner. "Think you can find your way back?"

Darcy shrugged noncommittally, her mind still on Jake's cat. "Thanks for dinner—and good luck with rehearsals."

"Yeah, I'll need it." He bared his teeth and then chuckled. "So what do you think? Can you see me with fangs?"

"A definite improvement," Darcy said, and he seemed to find it uproariously funny.

Hurrying back toward the laundry, Darcy's thoughts went in circles—Jake's cat . . . Elliott and his wild imagination . . . Elliott's prediction . . . Elliott's face. She could still *see* that face, even now, those scary dark glasses watching her from that alleyway.

Darcy stopped in midstride and glanced nervously behind her. *Come on, Darcy, why would Elliott be watching you? He hardly even knows you, and besides that, he's working at some gas station clear across town.* She was glad to see other people in the laundry. She waited restlessly for her clothes to dry, then hurried to get home.

She wasn't sure when she first suspected someone following her. And it was strange, she thought later, that even through all the noise on the streets, she could almost hear a certain pair of footsteps behind her, mocking her progress, step by step.

She didn't really know why she started running or why she was so frightened, knocking people out of her way as she searched frantically for a place to hide. Nothing looked familiar anymore. . . . She couldn't find the Dungeon—couldn't find Jake's club—and it was so dark now, on some strange street, and *Where did the people go, they were here just a second ago, I'm all alone—*

She saw an alley between two condemned buildings, and it looked so dangerous, so scary, but not nearly as scary as whatever was behind her, stalking her, knowing that she was too terrified now to turn around and look at it—

She flung herself into the narrow space, flattened

herself into the shadows, heart screaming, exploding in her chest.

The night was full of footsteps that never came.

As minutes passed Darcy's head began to clear. She fought off a wave of dizziness and realized she'd been holding her breath. Around her, shadows began to take shape and form—a brick wall . . . trash bags . . . a pile of old clothes . . .

She bent her head down to keep from fainting and saw a pale sliver of light angling in from some distant street lamp . . . slicing across the pile of old clothes. . . .

Only Darcy could see now that the clothes weren't old . . .

She could see that someone was still wearing them.

Someone . . . in a blood-soaked blouse . . . with blood-stained hair . . .

A girl . . . with a gaping slash across her throat.

**H**ere," Jake said. "Drink this."

Through blurry eyes Darcy saw a cup of coffee being shoved at her, but when she tried to take it, it spilled onto the table.

"She's still shaking." Jake's hand came into view, but another hand gently pried the cup from her fingers.

"That's okay, Darcy," Kyle said. "I've got it."

Around her the noises of the Club seemed strangely dreamlike. "I told them everything I know," Darcy mumbled. "Everything I saw."

"The cops are gone now." Jake leaned forward, peering anxiously into her face. "You might as well go home."

"Can't I stay here with you?" Her voice rose.

"Well, sure." Jake nodded. "Whatever you want."

"I could take her home," Kyle suggested.

"You get onstage," Jake said. "You're already late starting. And you guys quit arguing up there—it looks bad."

"Darcy"—Kyle patted her arm—"are you going to be okay?"

"Of course she is." Jake nudged him. "Go on, now."

Darcy reached for her coffee and tried another sip.

"So," Jake said, "someone was following you."

"No . . . I mean—I don't know. I guess not."

Jake threw up his hands. "So which is it?"

"I thought someone was. But they weren't. Or maybe they went away."

"But you didn't see anyone, right? No one you recognized?" He leaned forward, his voice urgent.

"No."

"What were you doing way over on that block anyway? It's not even near the apartment—"

"I got lost, okay?" Darcy's voice trembled, threatening to break. "I didn't know where I was! Everything looks different at night! I've only been here one day!"

"Yeah, you're right," Jake said matter-of-factly. "So don't cry."

Darcy turned away from him, her heart sinking as she saw Liz making her way over to their table.

"I heard what happened," Liz announced, and Darcy had the instant impression of being blamed for the whole horrible incident. "What'd she look like?"

"Dead," Darcy retorted before she could help herself, and shuddered at the memory.

"That was really stupid of you to be out wandering around alone," Liz said, sitting down in Kyle's vacated chair.

"I was getting my laundry." Darcy tried to compose herself. "Before that I wasn't alone. I was with Brandon and Kyle."

"Really." Liz's tone went icy, and Darcy stood up, looking appealingly at Jake.

"Could we please go home now?"

"I'm surprised you even remembered where I was," Jake said, "considering the state you were in."

"I didn't. I told the policeman I was your niece, and he knew where to find you."

"My cousin Tony." Liz nodded. "He said you were really freaking out."

Darcy turned away and felt Jake's hand on her elbow.

"I can't get away right now, Darcy. I've got someone waiting in my office, but I'll be done in about an hour."

"I'll go home with her," Liz said.

"I can wait," Darcy said firmly. "I'll just sit here till Jake's through."

"Brandon's picking me up here," Liz said, and Darcy could hear the smugness in her voice.

"Go on with Liz," Jake said. "No sense waiting around this place—"

"We can dump her on our way"—Liz raised an eyebrow—"unless, of course, she needs a babysitter at the apartment."

"That won't be necessary." Darcy's smile was stiff, and she followed Liz out onto the street. Brandon pulled up almost immediately, and Liz jumped in beside him while Darcy collapsed in the backseat. As Liz filled Brandon in on the latest murder, Darcy could see his worried glances in the rearview mirror.

"God, Darcy, are you all right?" He sounded shaken, but Liz brushed him off.

"She's fine. We're dropping her off, and then *we're* going to that movie you've been promising to take me to all week. And I can stay out *late*, remember? Since I don't have a *job* to go to anymore."

Brandon ignored her remark, his eyes darting between the mirror and the road. "Well, is Jake home? I mean, we can't just leave Darcy there by herself."

"She's a big girl," Liz retorted. "She's used to taking care of herself, aren't you, Darcy?"

Darcy was too drained to answer. To her surprise, it was Brandon who accepted Liz's challenge.

"Lay off, Liz. Can't you see she's upset?"

"Upset?" The sound in Liz's throat wasn't pleasant. "I don't know why she's so upset—walking around alone after dark, she was just asking for trouble. She's just lucky *she* didn't end up in some alley like that other girl."

"God, Liz." There was no mistaking the disgust in Brandon's tone. As the car pulled to the curb, Darcy got out at once, managing a feeble smile in Brandon's direction.

"Thanks. I really appreciate it."

His eyes looked anxious and sad. "Hey . . . no problem."

"Let's *go!*" Liz gave him a push. "I *hate* missing the start of a movie!"

"Maybe we should go in with her," Brandon stalled. "Just check out the place—"

"You don't want to be late." Darcy stepped back quickly, finding the idea of a dark apartment more appealing at the moment than this argument brewing in front of her. "Have fun, okay?"

Brandon's expression didn't look hopeful as they drove away. Darcy let herself into the brightly lit lobby, then leaned back against the door with a groan. She could still see that heap of rumpled clothing in the alleyway . . . that one hand clawing out in a last reach of panic. Her mind blanked out, and she tried to focus on the room around her . . . counter . . . souvenirs . . . posters . . . beaded curtain . . .

Her eyes glided past it, but a soft tinkling sound brought them back again. She stared at the long red ropes of glass and saw them shimmer. . . .

*Those beads are moving.*

Catching her breath, Darcy molded her spine to the door, pressed her palms flat against the wood. She saw the lobby as if she were watching from somewhere else—a casual observer from some other, safer dimension. She saw the bloodred beads stirring so softly that it might have been only a whisper that moved them . . . only a breath.

The air-conditioning, Darcy thought, and it was such a silly, unexpected thought that she felt her lips move in a wry smile. *Of course, that's it . . . the air-conditioning just kicked on . . . or it's just some draft in this old building. . . .* Yet she felt her feet moving forward . . . saw the strands of glass part with a cautious touch of her hand . . . heard herself call out, "Elliott, is that you?"

The tunnel beyond was all darkness.

Frozen there in the doorway, Darcy's mind catapulted between options—*call the police . . . run upstairs and lock myself in . . . get to the Club as fast as I can. . . .* "Elliott?" she called again. "Are you in there?"

Her voice floated down the labyrinth of hallways, fading into the unknown. Overhead the ceiling lights cast only a feeble glow. She took several steps and searched for a lightswitch. Damp walls slid beneath her fingertips. She paused as yet another tunnel curved before her and felt her heart slide slowly into her throat.

From somewhere down the darkness came a faint illumination, as if one of the exhibit spotlights had been left on.

"Elliott?" Darcy said hoarsely, but *Elliott's not here, he's working across town, and he's gone off, and forgotten to turn off one of the lights. . . .*

She squinted, trying hard to pierce the gloom along the passage, but the faint glow drew her on in a mixture of curiosity and fear. *If you were home and lights were on, what would you do?*

*I'd get ahold of myself and go turn them off.*

Annoyed now at her own cowardice, Darcy continued on, trying not to think about the ghoulish faces that watched her from the dark. As she stepped out into another chamber, she saw that one of the exhibits had indeed been left illuminated.

Count Dracula.

It was his eyes, she decided then, his eyes, so black, so commanding, so horribly lifelike in their pitiless seduction. Like the doomed woman in his arms, Darcy felt powerless to look away, mesmerized not only by his cruel intensity, but also by her own knowledge of vampire myths and legends. With an effort she finally pulled her eyes from his pale face, thinking how realistic it looked in the camouflage of light and shadow. Her gaze moved over the coffin—a *real* coffin—with smooth satin lining and brass handles that shone dully from one gloomy corner. And there were Dracula's feet, the toes of his black boots showing beneath the hem of his cape, and the bloodred lining, and upon one of his slender fingers a ring with a bloodred stone. As her eyes lingered upon that ring, she could almost swear that it winked at her, that some subtle movement, some unseen flick of the vampire's wrist had caused it to catch the half light . . . had caused it to shimmer . . . as the red-beaded curtain had shimmered. . . .

A cold-blooded snake of fear coiled slowly along Darcy's spine. She shifted her eyes to the dark ones of the vampire . . . black, shiny, glass eyes . . . and yet they seemed to mock her with an almost human glow of triumph. . . .

With a gasp she stepped back, not able to look at him anymore . . . just wanting to get away from those horrible, sadistic eyes—

There was no warning when the lights went out.

In front of her the stage went black . . . around her the chamber swallowed her alive.

With a scream Darcy backed into nothingness—

And felt strong, slow fingers curling around her neck.

Damn it, Darcy, is that you?"

Somewhere through her screams she recognized Jake's voice. At the same instant the pressure slid from around her neck.

"Jake? Where are you!" As the lights glared on, she put a hand to her eyes and tried to follow the sound of his voice.

"What are you doing in here?" Jake sounded annoyed. "You scared the *hell* out of me!"

"I scared *you!*" Relief and anger surged through her, and she blinked against the light, searching the walls . . . the doorways . . .

Jake pointed at the stage. "There shouldn't be any spotlights on back—"

Darcy didn't wait for him to finish. "I saw it, too, that's why I came in. I guess Elliott forgot this one when he left."

Jake shook his head. "That's not like Elliott."

"And why did you grab me anyway? You scared me to death."

"I didn't grab you. I wasn't even near you."

"Well, something did," Darcy said and watched Jake's eyes shift from Dracula to her face.

"How could anyone have grabbed you? There's no one here but you and me."

"But I felt it. Something around my neck."

"You must have imagined it."

"I didn't imagine it!"

"Come on, you just found a stiff in an alley— you're bound to be a little jumpy, huh?"

Darcy hesitated, confused. "Are you sure someone couldn't have gotten in here?"

"Not likely." Jake shrugged, then came slowly to her side, reaching up to a spot near the ceiling that she couldn't quite see.

"Here's the culprit." He drew down a handful of cobwebs and shook them onto the floor. "I've got to get this place really cleaned up soon."

"It wasn't cobwebs," Darcy insisted shakily. "It was solid. And smooth, not sticky."

Jake gave her that indifferent look she was beginning to recognize so well. "Darcy, it *had* to be cobwebs. What *else* could it be?"

Her eyes darted around the chamber, over the scattered shadows. "It felt . . . alive. Human. Like fingers."

"Fingers. . . ." Jake nodded and raised his arms, gesturing collectively at the exhibits in the room. "They come to life, you know. At night. After closing time."

Darcy didn't know whether to laugh or be furious with him. "It's creepy in here. I don't like it."

"And now you've hurt their feelings." Jake sighed, but he nudged her toward the tunnel. "Go on. I'm right behind you."

Darcy was relieved to get out of the Dungeon. While Jake rummaged through his office, she stood by, trying to calm her shattered nerves.

"How come you're here? I thought you had a meeting."

"Yeah," Jake said without looking up. "Funny, right? When I got to my office, the guy was gone. I just came back to pick up some stuff. Business."

"Oh." She'd been hoping he was home for the night and tried to hide her disappointment. "Well . . . then . . . good night."

"Yeah," Jake mumbled. "See you."

Her room was sweltering. Darcy raised the window and turned out her light, sitting there in the muggy darkness, listening to the night sounds below. Her head felt so heavy, and she leaned against the wall, wanting nothing more than to sleep. *It's all the excitement,* she argued with herself, *finding that body . . . and the Dungeon, that light going off . . . I know I felt something around my neck, but Jake's right, it couldn't have been anyone, and it's so hot in here, this terrible, sticky heat, I can hardly keep my eyes open. . . .* She squeezed her eyes tight, trying to keep all her grisly thoughts from forcing their way into her mind. *That poor girl and her look of terror . . . of surprise. . . .*

She didn't even get undressed. She fell onto the bed and was instantly asleep.

\*   \*   \*

"Darcy . . ."

"I'm awake, Mom." Groggily Darcy turned over and groped for her alarm clock, her hand swishing empty air. With a low groan she reached again, and as her eyelids struggled open, she suddenly realized that the unfamiliar darkness wasn't her old room at all. *Of course. I'm at Uncle Jake's. I must have been dreaming. . . .*

"Darcy . . ."

The voice came again, soft . . . eerie . . . Darcy raised her head from the pillow and froze.

As the voice whispered her name a third time, she saw a subtle darkening at the window, as if shadows had gathered just outside.

Something scratched at the screen.

Something . . . trying to get in.

In paralyzed horror, Darcy saw the outline of a hand working at the edge of the sill . . . heard the soft scraping of fingers against metal. . . .

She tried to scream but couldn't.

Helplessly she saw the fingers groping across her window . . . like quick black worms squirming out of the night. . . .

She scooted back against the wall, her mouth open in a soundless cry.

The fingers froze, like outstretched claws.

And as the hand pulled back into the darkness, something glittered at her and disappeared.

She saw it in that split second, a glimmer of red.

Something—*someone*—watching her with his bloodshot eye.

Darcy couldn't believe the time when she finally woke up the next morning—nine-thirty and hardly any time to spare before the Dungeon opened. As she rolled out of bed, she remembered her nightmare and moaned softly. Such a horrible dream— a prowler with red eyes, scratching at her window, calling her by name. . . . She massaged her temples gently, then crossed to the window to look out.

The first thing she saw were the rips in the screen.

Numbly Darcy stared at the jagged tears and then noticed one lower corner where the screen had been pulled away from its frame. *My God . . . I wasn't dreaming . . . something was trying to get in. . . .*

After throwing on her clothes, she raced downstairs, but Jake was nowhere around. As she came out into the lobby, she found Kyle and Elliott lounging on the counter, sharing a bag of jelly doughnuts, but the conversation stopped as she stared at them.

"Have you seen Jake?" She was trying to act normal, but Kyle was giving her a funny look. Elliott had no expression at all.

"He's probably at the Club," Kyle said helpfully. "You can call him . . . or I can run you by."

"You must have had nightmares," Elliott said softly. "You have that look . . . that bad-dream sort of face."

Darcy glanced at him sharply. "How do you know that, Elliott?"

The boy moved slowly down the counter, putting distance between them. When he didn't answer, Kyle spoke up.

"His mom's been sick a long time. She has lots of nightmares."

"She's dying," Elliott said to no one in particular.

At Darcy's look of alarm, Kyle shrugged sympathetically. "She has cancer," he mumbled.

"Oh, Elliott . . . I'm . . . I'm so sorry. . . ."

"He doesn't like to talk about it," Kyle said quickly. "So what's up?"

"Someone was trying to get in my room last night." Darcy tried to shift her attention back. "Trying to get in my window."

Elliott turned away from her and seemed to be staring at the beaded curtain. Kyle shifted awkwardly.

"But it was just a dream," he echoed, "like Elliott said."

"I don't know. I don't think so." Darcy leaned on the counter, her voice anxious. "I checked my screen when I woke up, and it's torn. And I thought . . ." Remembering the red eye glittering in at her, she gave a shudder. "I thought I saw someone looking in at me."

For a moment there was silence. Kyle glanced over at Elliott, but Elliott's attention remained on the entrance to the Dungeon.

"Did you tell Jake?" Kyle asked quietly.

"No, that's why I was looking for him."

"Your room's in the attic," Elliott said, and Darcy moved toward him.

"How did you know that?"

Elliott was still fixated on the curtain. His mouth moved several times before any words came out.

"Nobody could get up that high. They'd have to be able to fly to get up that high."

"Do you want me to have a look?" Kyle asked, stepping between them.

"Would you mind?" Darcy looked relieved, and she started for the stairs, turning again as a thought came into her mind.

"Oh, Elliott, you forgot to turn one of the lights off last night."

Finally Elliott moved, pulling himself slowly away from the beads to face her.

"No, I didn't."

"Well . . ." Darcy said uneasily, "I know you probably didn't mean to, but the Dracula exhibit was all—"

"I didn't forget," Elliott said. "I never forget that."

"It's okay." Kyle held up one hand, using the other to nudge Darcy up the stairs. "Just show me where this window is."

Darcy led the way up to her bedroom, unsettled by Elliott's behavior. "Is he always this weird?"

"Yes. But he's harmless."

"Are you sure about that?"

Kyle seemed amused by her suspicions. "Well, I guess you can't ever be a hundred percent sure about anybody, can you?" He examined the window, then stood aside, running one hand back through his hair.

"So what do you think?" Darcy asked nervously.

"Well . . ." He brushed one fingertip along one of the tears. "It's hard to say. This old screen's not in very great shape to begin with. You didn't notice how it looked before?"

She shook her head, gesturing toward the bottom corner. "He . . . it . . . was pulling from here. I saw his hands. Fingers. He was working very fast."

Kyle nodded distractedly and peered out, scanning the ground below. "There's an alley right under you. And no way up that I can see. I guess"—he shrugged apologetically—"you must have had a bad dream." As Darcy looked uncertain, he frowned and fanned himself. "It's a wonder you don't have heatstroke, it's so hot up here. Maybe *that's* what caused your dream."

"Maybe." Darcy sighed. "But I guess you're right. I guess no one could get up here. Thanks, anyway."

"No problem." He led the way back downstairs, pausing in the lobby. "By the way, there's a concert in the park tomorrow night we're all going to. Would you like to come?"

"All of you?" Darcy thought of Liz . . . and of Brandon.

"I mean, except for Elliott. He has to work."

"Are you sure I'd be welcome?"

His eyes crinkled up in that contagious smile. "Of course you'd be welcome. We'd really like you to go."

"Even Liz?" It was supposed to be a joke, but Kyle looked uncomfortable.

"Look . . . don't pay attention to Liz. I mean, none of us do."

As if on cue, they heard Liz's strident voice from the Dungeon, and a second later she practically fell into the room, Elliott appearing through the beaded curtain behind her.

"I can't let you in the workroom, Liz," Elliott said, his voice anxious. "I can't let you. You don't work here anymore."

"Like your new job, Darcy?" Liz's smile was

ice. "Would you mind ordering this imbecile to stop shoving me around?"

"Elliott—" Darcy began. "Liz—I—" She took a step forward, but it was Kyle who cut her off.

"Come on, Liz, lighten up. You know it's not Darcy's fault."

"Oh, really?" Liz folded her arms over her chest and looked daggers at him as he started for the door. "You're always for the underdog, aren't you, Kyle? Poor abandoned little Darcy."

Kyle stopped, but he didn't turn around.

"Let's just drop it, okay?" he said slowly. "It's Jake's place, he can do what he wants." He slammed the door as he went outside, and Liz stalked off again into the Dungeon.

"Liz!" Darcy called miserably. "Where are you going?"

"To get my things out of the workshop—*if* you don't mind—and *if* Elliott doesn't mangle me first—"

"Please wait! Please let's talk about this!"

"There's nothing I can see that needs talking about." From the way Liz made her way through the dim tunnels, Darcy could tell she'd done it many times before. "You have a job, and I don't. You're *special*, and I'm not. That's the breaks. I just want my stuff back, okay?"

"I didn't ask for the job!" Darcy tried to keep up. "I don't even *want* the job! You can have it back, I'll just tell Jake—"

"Hey, Darcy"—Liz spun around, her face mocking—"don't do me any favors, okay? I can get my own job."

"That's not what I—" Helplessly Darcy watched

Liz take off again and vanish down the corridors. "Damn!" She hit her fist against a guardrail and realized that she was at the Dracula exhibit again. "Well, Count," she said with a sigh, "seems like I always end up with you. We've really got to stop meeting like—"

The joke died in her throat.

Narrowing her eyes, she moved closer to the stage, letting her gaze travel slowly over the vampire's long, black cape.

*Something's different.*

She didn't know, really, how she knew—it just came to her in an odd sort of feeling that the scene was slightly off-balance and incomplete. She stepped closer, inspecting Dracula from his shiny boots up to his glassy eyes.

*Those eyes . . .*

Feeling a prickle along her scalp, Darcy stared into the Count's lifeless eyes, then at his white teeth . . . and then at the graceful, ruthless fingers trapping his victim.

*Something . . . something's different. . . .*

*Something's missing.*

And suddenly she knew, and her eyes riveted on his long, tapered finger where the red stone ring had glittered at her last night. . . .

*The ring.*

But he wasn't wearing the ring now.

And again she saw those fingers at her window . . . the fingers in her nightmare . . . and the blood-shot eye glimmering in at her . . . *the bloodstone ring.*

It hadn't been an eye at all.

And the fingers *had* been real.

# 10

Darcy leaned closer to the tableau, her eyes scanning the floor . . . the props . . . the thick shadows. *It must be here somewhere . . . maybe it fell off . . . got lost somehow.* She hurried back through the tunnels and met Elliott coming the other way.

"Elliott"—she stopped him—"I think something's missing from the Dracula exhibit."

He stood perfectly still. For a long time he stared at her as if he hadn't comprehended what she'd said.

"Did you hear me?" Darcy tried again. "Something is *missing*. I think it might have been stolen."

Elliott moved his head slowly from side to side. "That can't happen. I watch."

"I know you do, but I remember seeing a ring there yesterday, and now it's gone."

"What ring?"

Darcy's mouth dropped open. "Don't play games with me, Elliott—the ring Dracula was wearing."

Elliott was still shaking his head in that maddening way. "Ring?"

"The ring that's not there," she said impatiently. "The ring that was there yesterday but isn't there now. Please, Elliott, I know I didn't imagine it. A stone, about this big—red—very pretty."

In answer he shrugged and went past her, then suddenly turned around again.

"Maybe you dreamed about the ring," he said quietly.

Darcy felt herself bristling. "I didn't dream it! Why would you even say that?"

Again Elliot shook his head. "I don't know about any ring," he said and disappeared into the darkness of the tunnels.

There was little time to think about the ring after that—with a constant stream of visitors throughout the day, Darcy had her hands full and didn't see Elliott again until he mumbled goodbye and ducked out the door at closing time.

"Wait, Elliott, what about the—" Before Darcy could catch him, he was gone. She hurried outside and peered down the empty sidewalk, frowning. *How can anyone disappear so fast?* Locking up, she went upstairs just in time to catch the phone before it stopped ringing.

"Darcy?" a familiar voice greeted her. "This is Kyle. We're all going to meet here at the Club in a couple hours—why don't you come?"

"Well . . ." She was so tired, but the thought of

companionship overcame her aching body. "That sounds like fun," she agreed. "Thanks for asking me."

"Well, don't try to walk over here alone," Kyle added. "One of us will come get you."

Darcy felt a surge of relief that she hadn't expected. "I'll be here," she promised.

"Great. See you."

Up in her room Darcy flipped on the light and stared across at the window. It was all coming back to her again—her horrible dream-fantasy . . . the hand clawing at the screen . . . that eye—*no, that ring.*

Going closer, she reached out and touched the screen, her fingers sliding from top to bottom. *I didn't dream it, did I? There was a hand here, and Dracula's ring is missing, isn't it?* She leaned close to the window and looked down. *Just an alley, like Kyle said. A sheer drop to the ground. So how could anyone have possibly been at my window?*

On a sudden impulse Darcy turned and hurried downstairs. Clicking back the latch on the lobby door, she made sure she couldn't lock herself out, then stood out on the sidewalk and stared up at the old building. Blank walls and black windows stared back at her.

The side street was deserted and still. At the corner of the building she stopped and looked into the cramped little alley that crouched below her attic room. It was so dark in there . . . *too dark* . . . and as she carefully moved forward, shadows pressed in from all sides, as if trying to suffocate her. She stopped directly below her window and gazed up the straight brick walls, shaking her head in bewilderment. *I must have dreamed it.* . . . And then she spotted something.

About three feet ahead of her a tall fence rose up, dead-ending the alleyway, but between the fence and the building lay a dark, narrow space and something else that jutted out from the lower corner of the building.

It looked like a step.

Cautiously Darcy approached it, holding her breath as she peeked around the corner.

It *was* a step. The bottom step of a fire escape that crawled up the back wall.

Heart pounding, she took hold of the railing and began to climb the metal stairs, but when she reached the small landing, the door she found there was locked. Remembering back, her mind sketched a quick floor plan of the apartment, and her grip slowly tightened on the railing.

The door had to open to Jake's bedroom.

Darcy leaned against the wall and tried to think. *When Jake showed me around the apartment, he never showed me his own room . . . was it because of this door?* Frowning, she stared down at the fire escape again. *But this still doesn't explain how someone could climb up to my window.*

She tilted her head back and carefully scanned the side of the building. Then slowly her eyes widened.

She hadn't noticed the ledge before. Because of its design and identical color of the building, it had merely seemed like part of the wall as she'd stared up at it from the alley. But now . . . now she could see that it was just wide enough for feet to stand on . . . positioned so that someone standing there

could easily reach her window if they stretched . . .
if they were tall. . . .

A cold lump formed in her chest, and her gaze
swept up again. *There*. There right in front of her—
*that's how he got up to that ledge*. And she ran
her hands over the uneven bricks in the corner
section of the wall . . . bricks uneven enough to
be footholds and handholds *so that someone could
boost himself up and work his way along the ledge
and pry open my window. . . .*

Swallowing a cry, Darcy scrambled back down
the fire escape telling herself she was being stupid,
that it was impossible—*impossible!*—and why
would *anyone* want to get inside her room, why
would *anyone* want to hurt her—and *What's the
matter with you, you're getting hysterical, starting
to imagine all sorts of crazy things, stop it right
now, so you found some steps—a ledge—it doesn't
mean anything, not anything at all—*

She reached the front door and rammed her
shoulder against it, suddenly desperate to get
inside. She turned the handle and pushed, and then
with a gasp of disbelief, she twisted and pushed
again.

The door was locked.

**11**

*This can't be happening—I was so careful—I know I checked to make sure it was open—*

Darcy pounded with her fists, but the sound echoed down the street, mocking her. Taking a deep breath, she stepped back and scanned the sidewalk with worried eyes. The wind? *But there's hardly a breeze, and that couldn't have affected the latch.* . . . She thought about finding a pay phone . . . trying to walk to the Club . . . but the twilight seemed full of hidden dangers, and without warning the face of the dead girl in the alley floated into her mind. *I've got to do something—I can't just stay here all night.*

As Darcy stood there in frustration, trying to decide what to do, the lights in the lobby flickered and went off. Startled, she knocked again, straining her ears for some answer to her shouts.

"Jake! Is that you? It's me, Darcy! I've locked myself out!"

The lights came back on.

Breathing a sigh of relief, Darcy waited for the door to open.

Nothing happened.

"Jake?" Again she knocked, a knot of fear twisting in her stomach. "Come on, it's scary out here!"

Only silence answered her. Darcy stepped back and glanced nervously around at the darkness. *There must be some other way in. . . .*

She began searching for another entrance, heading in the opposite direction from where she'd gone before. As she moved cautiously along the side of the building, she was almost past the basement window before she even noticed it, hidden there behind months of trash and grime. Kneeling down, she was surprised that it opened so easily, and she held her breath, lowering herself inside.

For an endless moment Darcy hung there, suspended in nothingness, legs groping for a foothold. And then, as her shoes found something solid, she eased herself down, squinting into thick shadows that swirled around her. She could make out walls now, and a door, but when she tried the knob, it wouldn't budge.

"Jake!" Again Darcy began to pound, praying her voice would carry upstairs. "I'm in the basement! Come on—let me out!"

And then she heard the footsteps.

With a surge of relief Darcy prepared to knock again . . . and then her hand froze in midair.

The steps weren't coming from the other side of the door.

They were outside the basement window.

Choking off a cry, Darcy dropped to her knees and huddled down in the shadows. From out in the alley the steps came closer . . . closer . . . sharp against the pavement . . . slow . . . and deliberate.

They were taking their time.

Trembling now, Darcy wrapped her arms about herself and tried to make herself smaller. She sensed a movement beside her and bit down on her fist, as a mouse, and then another, scurried across her ankles.

The footsteps had reached the window now.

In slow-motion horror Darcy saw a shape glide past the opening. Holding her breath, she curled herself into the corner and closed her eyes.

The sounds stopped.

The silence went on and on.

Very slowly Darcy's eyes began to open . . .

Just in time to see the shoes climbing in through the window.

She couldn't even scream. In a haze of paralyzing fear, Darcy saw the feet descending . . . the long, black folds of a cape billowing down into the darkness. . . .

She saw a glint of silver, razor sharp, as it slid through the shadows—

"*No!*" she shrieked. "*No! Oh, God—no—*"

She flung herself upon the door, beating with her fists, crying at the top of her lungs, and it was a nightmare, a whole horrible dream with no escape, and it went on forever—*forever*—until the door burst open without warning, and she fell out into a pair of arms that wrestled her to the floor as she fought them.

"Cut it out, Darcy! It's me—it's *me!*"

As Darcy twisted herself out of reach, she blinked up into a flashlight and Brandon's bewildered face.

"Oh, God . . . oh, Brandon—is that you?"

"Of course it's me. Who'd you think it was?"

"I don't know—I—I—" Her knees buckled, and she sat down hard upon the floor.

"What are you *doing* down here? How'd you get in?" Brandon sounded angry now, and as she gazed up at him, something inside of her snapped.

"Didn't you *see* him? You *had* to see him—he was right behind me—we have to call the police, Brandon, we—"

"What are you talking about? Who was behind you?"

Darcy stared at him stupidly, her mind refusing to function.

"Didn't you see him? Didn't you hear him?"

*"Who?"* Brandon demanded. "The only one I heard was *you!* What are you trying to do—wake the dead?"

"The dead?" Darcy mumbled. "I almost *was* dead, Brandon, I almost *was*—I mean—he was right over there—"

Brandon knelt beside her, frowning. "Come on, Darcy, whatever you thought you saw is gone now. Look—there's nobody here but us. You must have just—"

"Don't you dare tell me I imagined this." Darcy glared at him. "Don't you dare. Someone came in the window after me—you must have scared him off. He had a . . . a knife—or something—he was—"

"Come on." Brandon slid his hands beneath her elbows and lifted her to her feet. "Now, what the hell are you doing down here? Jake never uses this old storeroom anymore—you're lucky I even heard you at all."

"I got locked out, but I saw the lights, and I thought Jake was home, so I found this window. . . ." She studied him, eyes narrowed. "What are *you* doing here? Where's Jake?"

"How should I know where Jake is?" Brandon drew himself up indignantly. "I came to pick you up, and the front door was unlocked and you were gone. I didn't know what to think!"

Darcy hesitated, letting his words sink in. "So—so you really didn't see anyone outside?"

"Not a soul."

"Well"—her voice rose nervously—"you don't think he got inside, do you? You don't think he's hiding somewhere in the building, do you? In the Dungeon?"

"Not unless he has a key." Brandon sighed. "But, okay, I'll look around." He pulled her toward him and steadied her shoulders. "Wait in the lobby for me."

"No, Brandon, please, why can't we just call the police? I don't want you to go in the Dungeon—"

"You act like they're all going to come to life and come after me."

Darcy flushed and said nothing as they went upstairs. While she waited beside the phone in

Jake's office, Brandon went to investigate the tunnels.

"So?" Darcy was relieved when he came back. "Did you find anything?"

Brandon gave a solemn nod, hesitating at her frightened look. "I guess I should tell you," he said slowly, averting his eyes. "The Wolfman bit Mr. Hyde on the leg."

Darcy stared at him, feeling her cheeks redden. Without a word she turned and started up to the apartment.

"Hey, come on!" Brandon laughed, right on her heels. "It was just a joke! Hey! I'm sorry—"

She tried to close the door, but he blocked it with his shoulder.

"Hey!" Brandon struggled to keep a straight face. "I'm sorry, okay? Really—"

"No, you're not."

"I swear! Come on, Darcy, I'm just trying to make you feel better!"

"Then go away."

He caught her shoulders and turned her around to face him. "I shouldn't have made fun—I'm sorry, okay? Don't be mad. Now what *I* want to know is, what were you doing outside tonight in the first place?"

She slipped out of his grasp and moved to the window, staring down into the street, conscious of his body moving closer to her.

"Oh, you'll just think I'm being silly."

"Maybe not," he said, considering. "Maybe I'm really just one hell of an understanding guy."

A smile touched her lips, then faded.

"I think someone tried to break into my room last night."

His dark eyes held her. She felt the slight pressure of his body as he leaned forward.

"Yeah," he said softly. "Kyle told me about that."

"He did?" Darcy didn't know whether to feel relieved or embarrassed. "I'm not making it up, Brandon. I mean, at first I thought maybe I dreamed it—but then I went outside this evening to look. There's a fire escape behind the building and a ledge below my room. And the way the bricks are staggered in the wall, it'd be easy for someone to climb up."

"But why would they?" Brandon asked, matter-of-factly. "I mean . . . why would someone go to all that trouble?"

Darcy hesitated and looked away. After his earlier reaction, her ideas of vampires and bloodshot eyes and stone rings seemed preposterous, if not downright laughable. She shrugged, abruptly changing the subject.

"So why did *you* come tonight? I thought you had rehearsals."

Brandon looked surprised, then amused. "Oh, I get it—I'm a suspect."

Darcy turned away. "I just wondered, that's all."

"We finished up early. I was informed you needed an escort." His teasing changed to seriousness. "And about last night . . . your finding that body, I mean. . . . God, Darcy, that must have been awful for you. I wanted to stay with you for a while but . . ."

*But, Liz.* Darcy closed her eyes. "I'm not supposed to talk about it—the police don't want a panic on their hands. I guess . . . no one's heard anything else."

"Just that they're pretty sure it's the same killer. The Vampire." He grinned then and made a sweeping bow. "Enough drama for one night. Shall we go?"

"You do that very well," Darcy said grudgingly, going ahead of him down the stairs.

"Yeah? I keep telling myself, think suave, think charm . . . think sex."

"And I'm sure your powers of concentration are amazing." Darcy gave in to a laugh. "Are we walking or riding?"

"Perhaps I should wrap my cape around you, and we'll just fly." Brandon stopped on the sidewalk and struck a gallant pose. "I'm getting good at this, don't you think? I'm learning all kinds of interesting things."

"Such as?"

"Such as . . ." Brandon's arm curled lazily around her neck, drawing her close, so that they were walking side by side. "If a vampire drinks too much of his victim's blood, the victim dies. But mostly he just drinks enough to satisfy his— uh—thirst. The victim gets weaker and weaker and more and more under his power."

It had started to drizzle, a thin gray fog creeping along the streets. In spite of the warm night, Darcy shuddered and felt Brandon's arm tighten, pulling her closer.

"Can you imagine?" he said, with something

like wonder in his voice. "Can you imagine having that much power?"

"It's creepy," Darcy said flatly. "Do you really think about this stuff during rehearsals?"

"Well, an actor has to do whatever it takes to get in the mood, doesn't he?" Brandon grinned down at her. "There's more."

"Lucky me," Darcy groaned, but he was off again.

"And you know all those stories about vampires dying in the sun?"

Darcy nodded. "They scream and shrivel up, if I remember my horror movies."

"Well, not all of them do." He sounded almost smug. "Some vampires are immune to the sun. Which makes them even scarier, of course."

"Of course."

"I mean, if none of the standard vampire repellants work, then how do you get rid of the guy, huh?" He chuckled then, squeezing her gently against him, and she glanced up into his face.

"Do you think this Vampire—the killer, I mean—really believes he *is* one?"

Another couple passed them on the sidewalk—without warning Darcy found herself crushed up against Brandon's chest as the people shoved her aside. Brandon stopped and looked earnestly into her eyes.

"If he does, then that makes him extremely dangerous."

His tone was so solemn that Darcy felt another chill go through her.

"Why do you say that?"

"Because he can be any kind of vampire he

wants to be, so that makes him unpredictable. If he were a *real* vampire—a really *traditional* vampire—then they'd know how to catch and destroy him. But if he's making up the rules as he goes along . . ."

This time it was Brandon who shuddered, and he wrapped his arms tight around her, resting his chin on her head.

"No more vampire talk," he said softly. "Let's do something else. You like flowers?"

Darcy looked surprised. "Yes, but I thought we were going to the Club."

"They won't miss us for a while." Brandon checked his watch, nodding. "Kyle's getting ready to go on about now—he won't finish up for another half hour. Come on. I want to show you something."

She had no idea how far they'd gone when Brandon finally stopped and pointed. Ahead of them the buildings thinned out and disappeared, leaving a wide open stretch of bricked street, a city-block long, flanked on either side by wooden stalls and tables. In the hazy glow of streetlights, awnings fluttered and snapped in the wet breeze, and a heavy odor of overripe fruit sweetened the air.

"The Farmer's Market," Brandon announced, taking a deep breath. "Tomorrow morning this place will be so full you can hardly move through it. Come on."

"But there's nothing to see—" Darcy started to argue, but Brandon grabbed her arm and pulled.

They made their way past rows of deserted stands, their footsteps echoing unevenly on the cobbled pavement. Ethnic signs swung on rusty chains, groaning softly.

"Wait." Darcy stopped, and Brandon turned to face her. "Where are we going?"

Through the shadows she saw his half smile. "Wow. You really *don't* trust me, do you?"

Before she could answer, he started off again, a distorted silhouette in the mist.

"Wait!" Darcy called. For one second a wild thought stabbed through her mind—*He's leaving me here—something's going to happen—something bad*—and she started running, damp gray fingers of fog clinging to her clothes . . . her skin . . . "Brandon!" she cried. "Where are you?"

"Here," he said, and she stopped abruptly as his hand came out of the shadows.

He held a bouquet of red carnations.

"For you." He smiled.

In confusion Darcy searched the empty stalls but saw no one.

"Where did you get these?" Her voice was weak, trembling from fear and relief and bewilderment all at once, and he was still smiling at her, lifting one hand to her cheek.

"From the vendor back there . . . didn't you see her?"

"No—no, I didn't see anyone—" And still she strained her eyes through the fog, and his fingertips traced lightly over her cheekbone.

"Well," he said quietly. "Well . . . then, I guess she must have left."

Darcy looked deep into his eyes and thought she could lose herself in their blackness.

"You're shaking all over." Brandon's voice was deep and steady. "I didn't mean to scare you."

"Well, you did," she said, and the flowers were in her hand, and Brandon was wrapping her fingers around them, oh, so gently. "You really did scare me, Brandon."

"I'm sorry." And his lips closed over hers, a long sweet kiss, and he pressed her tightly against him. "I'm sorry, Darcy," he said again softly. "I'd never—ever—want to scare you."

## 12

*N*ice flowers," Kyle said, eyeing Darcy's carnations. "Bet you got them at the market."

"How'd you know?" Darcy glanced at him curiously. She laid her bouquet on the table and tried to move her chair farther away from the Club's crowded dance floor.

"Oh . . . let's just say it was a hunch," Kyle said. And then, almost as an afterthought, "Better not let Liz see them."

Darcy felt her heart sink, and Kyle turned away, trying not to smile. *I wonder how many times Brandon's bought flowers for Liz . . . or for how many other girls. . . .* She stared at the flowers, suddenly wishing she could slip them discreetly under her chair. When she lifted her eyes, Kyle was looking at her again, but then glanced off.

"Who's that guy at the bar?" Darcy whispered.

Kyle tried to turn inconspicuously. "What guy?"

"There. He keeps looking over here like he's watching me."

Kyle slid a glance in the stranger's direction, then leaned closer to Darcy. "I don't know . . . one of Jake's buddies, I guess. I've seen him in here before. . . . I've also seen Jake throw him out."

"He looks like a real creep."

"He probably is. Pretend you don't notice him, and maybe he'll leave." He turned back to her with a smile. "Still up for the concert tomorrow night?"

"Sure," Darcy said, not feeling up to it at all. She nodded an absentminded thanks to Brandon as he put a Coke down in front of her and slid into an empty chair.

"What concert?" Brandon asked, then snapped his fingers. "Oh, no! I forgot that jazz group was playing! And I've got a stupid rehearsal!"

"Just meet us there after," Kyle said. "They always run late."

"But I bet I'll miss most of it," Brandon grumbled.

"Ah, the sacrifices one must make for one's art." Kyle ducked as Brandon tried to punch him. "And speaking of art, how *is* the Count today?"

"Here I am, in all my . . . *gory.*" Brandon's eyebrows went up and down, and Kyle groaned.

"Your humor is too *grave* for me."

"Oh, yeah? Well, *fangs* a lot."

This time it was Darcy who groaned, and they both eyed her indignantly.

"Well, what's the matter with her? Some people would *die* for our company."

"Of *corpse.*"

Unable to stand it any longer, Darcy started to laugh, and the boys joined in. The next minute the table grew uncomfortably quiet as they all looked up to see Liz standing over them. Darcy felt an instant knot in her stomach and stared miserably at the wall, trying to make the flowers disappear through desperate wishing. Liz was staring at the carnations with a frosty smile.

"Yours?" she asked Darcy.

Darcy heard her own voice from a long way off. "Yes."

The other girl's smile grew colder and tighter. "How sweet. Kyle's always been the thoughtful one."

Darcy saw a muscle move in Kyle's cheek, but she couldn't tell if he was bracing himself for an attack or hiding a smile—or both.

"I went to the theater." Liz stared imperiously down at Brandon. "I didn't see you."

"I wasn't there," Brandon replied. "And those flowers aren't from Kyle."

Kyle pursed his lips in a silent whistle and fastened his gaze to a spot on the wall.

"I see." Liz's hand lowered to the top of Brandon's head, moved down the length of his ponytail . . . tightened . . . and steadily pulled. Brandon's head bent slowly backward until his eyes looked up into hers. "I think," Liz said icily, "we should talk."

Brandon's dark eyes flashed. He forced his lips into a mocking smile. "How about now?"

"That would be fine," Liz said sweetly.

Darcy looked away as Liz started for the door and Brandon pushed himself up from the table with a sigh.

"Just ask yourself," Kyle advised, "what Dracula would do in a situation like this."

Brandon rolled his eyes. "He wouldn't waste his appetite. She'd just be a quick hors d'oeuvre."

Kyle grinned over at Darcy as Brandon disappeared through the crowds.

"Wow. You've really made an enemy, and you haven't even tried." And then, at the look on her face, he leaned over, contrite. "Hey, I'm sorry. Believe me, it doesn't take *anything* for Liz to hate you. She doesn't have any friends."

Darcy felt both angry and near tears, and she took a long swallow of Coke. "Why does she act like that?"

" 'Cause she's the queen bee at home. My parents have made her believe she can have anything she wants and everything she doesn't have." He gave a tolerant smile and reached over and squeezed her shoulder. "You feel like riding?"

"Where?"

"I don't know. Anywhere. You like motorcycles?"

"I've never been on one. They look dangerous."

"Not mine." He stood up and pulled her to her feet. "Let's get out of here."

"But maybe I should tell Jake—"

"I'll tell him. Just wait for me by the door. Hey, don't you want your flowers?"

"Uhhh . . . actually they look really nice here. I think I'll leave them."

While Kyle headed off to Jake's office, Darcy pushed her way through the crowds and out the front entrance. The damp air felt good as she stood there on the sidewalk. Pulling her clothes away from her body, she fanned herself, turning her face up to the sky. A light drizzle still hung in the air, and the street lay around her, a gray illusion. She lifted her hair from her neck and let her eyes wander over the fog.

And then she saw him.

A thin face . . . lanky blond hair . . . the dark glasses like two deep holes where his eyes should have been . . .

"Elliott . . ."

She turned back and felt Kyle's arms go around her, and with a startled cry she jumped out of his grasp.

"Okay! Okay!" Kyle held up both hands, his eyes wide. "No touching! I promise!"

"No!" Darcy grabbed his arm and tugged him out to the curb, gesturing toward the foggy street. "Look! It's Elliott! Over there by that building!"

Kyle looked all around the deserted street and sidewalks, scratching his head. "Darcy—"

"He was here," Darcy said, dismayed. "He *was!* Just like he was there the *last* time you didn't see him!"

Kyle nodded, his shoulders moving in an amicable shrug. "I mean, Elliott's working—"

"Across town," Darcy finished. "At his night job. But what if he's not? What if he's not even there tonight? Then would you believe me?"

"Okay." Kyle began walking. "Okay, if it'll make you feel better. My bike's right over here.

We'll drive over to the station and see if Elliott's there.''

"No." Darcy stopped, shaking her head. "No, you're just humoring me."

Kyle thought a minute . . . ran one hand through his hair. "But, hey, wouldn't you love to prove me wrong? Liz *delights* in it."

Darcy stared at him, feeling a smile creep across her face. "Actually, I would."

"Spoken like a true female." Kyle grinned. "This way, m'lady. Your trusty steed awaits you."

"Steed?" Darcy laughed.

"Yeah." He looked down at her, poker-faced. "If it was Brandon, then it'd be your trusty stud, but since it's only my bike—"

She gave him a playful shove and followed him to where he'd parked.

It took about twenty minutes to go across town. As they pulled into the gas station, Darcy saw Elliott working in the garage, and her heart sank. Kyle stopped the bike, and Elliott came out, wiping his hands on a dirty rag.

"Hey, man," Kyle greeted him. "How's it going?"

"Okay," Elliott mumbled. He was staring at Darcy, but she ducked her head and pretended to examine the helmet she'd taken off.

"How come?" Elliott said.

"How come what?" Kyle returned pleasantly.

"You're here."

"Just showing Darcy around town." Kyle slid off and unscrewed the gas cap. "Realized I needed to feed this thing. Figured I'd stop and say hi."

The other boy nodded and turned toward Kyle, his thin hands working slowly . . . steadily . . . into the dirty rag they were holding. There was a long streak of grease down one of his cheeks, and sweat glistened on his high, wide forehead.

"I didn't leave that light on," he said to Darcy, and she glanced up in surprise.

"I didn't come here about that, Elliott." She shook her head. "Forget about it."

"You shouldn't be here," Elliott said, and Darcy jumped as he put his hand on her arm.

"She's with me," Kyle said easily.

"This is a bad part of town," Elliott went on patiently. "Murders happen here."

"It's okay," Kyle reassured him. "She's fine." He replaced the hose and dug into his pocket. "I need some change."

Elliott's head moved in the direction of the office, and Kyle mouthed "I'll hurry" as he started in. Darcy again concentrated on her helmet strap, but felt Elliott's hand return to her arm. When she looked up, he had taken his glasses off, and his wide, pale gray eyes were only inches from hers.

"I was right," he mumbled. "Wasn't I."

A coldness crept through her, yet she managed to hold his stare. "About what?"

"You know." His expression was blank. "The murder." One finger raised until it was level with her chin. "You know. It really happened."

"Elliott—"

"And I remembered. About the ring. Kyle and Brandon thought it would look good in Brandon's play. Maybe they took it."

"Are you talking about me?" Kyle clapped Elliott good-naturedly on the shoulder and winked at Darcy. "Some friend you are. I can't turn my back for a minute—"

"We were talking about rings," Darcy said. "Did Brandon borrow a ring from the Dracula exhibit?"

"No . . ." Kyle looked puzzled. "He decided he didn't want to use it after all."

"We were talking about murder," Elliott murmured. "You should believe me when I say things will happen."

Kyle saw Darcy's anxious face and shook his head with a patient smile. "No more talk about murder, okay, Elliott? No more talk about the future." He swung one leg over the bike and checked to make sure Darcy was holding on tight. "There's only one thing about Darcy's future we both know for sure, right, Elliott? That Brandon will find *some* way to be in it."

Elliott's mouth lifted tentatively at the corners, and he put his sunglasses back on. "I know *your* future, too. But you won't like it."

Kyle regarded him curiously and let out a soft groan. "I don't need this tonight . . . what is it?"

"They're auditioning a new drummer. I heard them talking about it."

Kyle leaned his head upon the handlebars and groaned even louder. "I knew this was going to happen! But why is it happening to me?"

"They don't know that I know."

Kyle sighed and looked up again. Darcy could see the hurt in his eyes.

"Are you positive?"

"I'm positive."

"Well, this ought to make my parents happy," Kyle said softly. He revved the motor and gave Elliott a sad smile. "Thanks, man. See you around."

Elliott stood there silently and watched them leave.

After a long while Kyle seemed to shake himself back to attention. "Satisfied?" he yelled back over his shoulder.

"About what?"

"Elliott."

"He could have gotten there ahead of us, couldn't he?" Darcy yelled back.

She felt him shrug, but he didn't answer, so she buried her head against his back. Through his T-shirt she could feel the hard flow of his muscles as he guided the motorcycle through town, and suddenly she didn't care where they were going— she didn't want to care about *anything*—she just nestled tighter against him as the misty night flowed over her, lulling her into a safe, easy calm.

Without warning the bike stopped, and Darcy lifted her head to peer over Kyle's shoulder. Ahead of her she could see a girl walking alone down the street, and it took her a minute to realize it was Liz. As Kyle pulled up alongside, his sister cast him a ferocious glare.

"What's going on?" Kyle asked. "Where's Brandon?"

"Get out of here!" Liz yelled. "Leave me alone!"

"Come on, Liz." Kyle kept up with her while Darcy looked on apprehensively. "You shouldn't be out here alone—where's Brandon?"

"How should I know! We had a fight in his car,

and the jerk let me off in the middle of nowhere! I've been walking for miles!"

"Liz—will you just stop—"

"He's probably hoping the Vampire gets me!" Liz seethed. "And wouldn't that make him happy if I got my throat cut—wouldn't that make him happy if I died—"

"Come on, don't talk like that—" Kyle reached out one arm, but she slapped it away.

"Just because I hit him!" she said furiously. "Well, he *deserved* it! I told him I wanted flowers, so we had a fight, and he *insulted* me—"

"Where is he now?"

"How should I know! Who *cares?* He had it coming!"

"I doubt that." Kyle sighed. "You're lucky he didn't decide to drop you *ten* miles from here."

Liz flew at him so fast that Darcy didn't see her coming. It was all Kyle could manage to keep the motorcycle upright.

"Cut it out, Liz, you're going to hurt someone!" Kyle yelled at her. "I ought to leave you here!"

"I *want* you to!" Liz yelled back at him. "I want you to leave me here so you'll feel guilty about it all *night!*"

Kyle glanced back at Darcy, shaking his head with a tolerant smile. "Okay, Liz, I'm going—"

"Fine! Just go!"

To Darcy's concern, Kyle sped off. For several more blocks they didn't speak, but as he turned onto a side street, she recognized the Farmer's Market. It didn't take long to find Brandon. As Kyle and Darcy approached a row of deserted stands, they saw him lying back on one of the wooden tables.

"Who won?" Kyle asked, deadpan, and Brandon looked up, raising a bottle in greeting.

Kyle squinted and laughed. "Are you drinking?"

"Just this awful grape stuff." Brandon sighed. "I couldn't handle anything stronger right now—not with this lump on my head."

Kyle stepped closer and whistled. "Wow—that's a beauty."

"I ended up clear in the backseat," Brandon said, almost admiringly. "Where'd she learn to punch like that?"

Kyle shrugged and sat beside him. "She's pretty mad."

"No kidding. *I'm* probably deformed."

"You'll live." Kyle took the bottle and helped himself to a sip. "Here's to women . . . and their charms."

"Well, hi, Darcy." Brandon noticed her at last. "So glad you could join us."

"Someone's stopping," Darcy said nervously, watching the street.

To her surprise, Jake and Elliott pulled up in a car and got out. While Elliott hung back, Jake towered over Brandon and gave him a hard appraisal.

"Why the hell did you call me?"

" 'Cause I was too dizzy to drive. And anyway, you're the only one I could get ahold of. God, Jake, I thought you'd be a lot more sympathetic than this."

Jake took Brandon's collar and hoisted him to his feet. "Come on—Elliott, you drive Brandon's car. Brandon, this is the last time, understand? I don't have time to referee all your and Liz's fights. Where is she?''

"I don't know. Walking somewhere—"

"Walking! With some maniac running loose? Elliott, go find her—"

"I know where she is," Kyle said. "You take Darcy home."

"And what are *you* going to do?"

Kyle shrugged. "Well, I know Liz won't let me give her a ride, so I guess I'll just follow her."

Brandon grinned. "Spoken like a true gentleman."

"Get in the car." Jake shoved him.

"Hey, I'm injured here—"

"He does have a pretty bad bump," Darcy spoke up, but Jake only looked more irritated.

"Get in the car, Darcy. You shouldn't be out here, either."

"What do you mean, she shouldn't be out here, either?" Brandon gave a chuckle. "She's with us, isn't she? You act like something's going to happen to her or something."

"What I'm saying is, anything could happen to anybody," Jake said shortly. "Especially after what's been happening these past few days."

Kyle glanced around at the empty stalls, the foggy walkways, the distorted shadows. "He's right, Brandon. I'm going to go catch Liz."

Brandon hesitated, then gave an exaggerated stage whisper. "Do you think the Vampire's back there somewhere? Hiding? Licking his lips? Sharpening his fangs? Watching? Picking out his next . . . terrified . . . victim—"

"Go on, Brandon," Jake gave him a shove. "Move!"

Back at the apartment once more Darcy checked and rechecked the locks, unable to shake a nagging feeling of dread. Jake had returned to the Club, and she hated the idea of being alone all night, especially when her brain kept going over and over all the troubling events of the day—*the fire escape . . . the basement window . . . but I know someone was there, coming after me, wanting to hurt me, and how long was I standing there calling for help? It seemed like forever. . . . How long until the intruder left and Brandon opened the door . . .*

She knew Brandon hadn't believed her. And now she began to suspect that the flowers hadn't meant anything at all, that maybe he'd only been patronizing her. . . . *Brandon is obviously a huge flirt, and Liz is obviously very used to having her own way, and you are so stupid for presuming anything or even wishing for it.*

She couldn't sleep. She tossed restlessly in the sticky heat and kept looking at her watch, wondering when Jake would be home. She couldn't stop thinking about all the things Brandon had said back there at the Farmer's Market.

"Do you think the Vampire's back there somewhere?" he had joked, thinking it so clever and oh-so-funny. . . .

*"Picking out his next terrified victim?"*

*And how horrible,* Darcy thought, pressing her face tight into her pillow, trying to choke back the awful fear—*how horrible to be the next victim . . .*

*And never know your life was running out so fast. . . .*

# 13

When Darcy heard the whispers, she thought at first she was dreaming . . . voices low and urgent . . . bodies moving quickly . . . quietly through the dark.

She sat up, heart racing. She listened hard through the blackness and thought a door closed somewhere downstairs. Peeking out her room and down the stairwell she saw the lamp she'd left burning below . . . and once again she thought she heard muffled voices. She slipped noiselessly down to the living room and saw a sliver of light beneath Jake's door.

Standing there, Darcy tried to decide if she should investigate, then froze as the door slid open a crack, letting out soft voices from within.

"I almost got it this time—this was the worst—"

"Ssh . . . you'll wake Darcy. . . ."

Still whispering, the voices were unrecognizable to her, but then the first one came again, bordering on panic.

"I didn't expect it—the struggle—oh, God—"

Holding her breath, Darcy saw Jake move into her line of vision, saw him holding something . . . saw him throw it into his closet. His clothes were torn and bloody, and there was more blood streaming down from his hand. He was talking to someone that Darcy couldn't see, and as the closet door groaned shut, he moved out of sight again.

She heard someone speaking—*Who? Jake? Who else is in there?*—but only caught the end of what was being said.

"—have to take care of her."

Darcy felt a stab of terror. There was a loud thud as if someone had collapsed against a wall, and then another muffled cry, broken and anguished.

"I can't stand this anymore! Oh, God, what am I going to do!"

Darcy didn't wait to hear anything else; she fled upstairs and locked herself in.

The night crawled on and on, and she lay awake, eyes fixed on the ceiling. *My God, Jake, what's going on?* For a long time there wasn't another sound from downstairs, then finally a door opened and closed as an invisible someone left the apartment. She thought she might have drifted off to sleep at last when suddenly the phone rang, jarring her awake, and Jake's voice drifted up, strangely calm.

"Darcy, it's for you."

"Me?" She swung out of bed, put her ear timidly to the door. "For me?"

But he didn't answer, and she heard the sound of his bedroom door. For the second time that night she peeked cautiously down the stairwell, then hurried to the living room where the receiver lay upon a table beside the couch.

"Hello?" she whispered.

"Darcy? I can hardly hear you."

She recognized the voice and sank into the cushions. "Oh, Brandon," she said gratefully.

"What's the matter? You acted like this was going to be obscene or something." His voice smiled. "Hey . . . I really wanted to get back tonight to see you. It . . . just didn't work out."

*So you and Liz fixed things. Good for you, bad for me.* "Well, I hope everything's okay now."

"That depends on your point of view, I guess," he said vaguely. "I had fun on our walk this evening. Yours and mine, I mean."

"Me, too." *Well, I might as well be honest, it'll probably be the last walk we ever take.*

"I'll try and make it to the concert tomorrow night—it just depends on rehearsals. Maybe I'll see you."

"Maybe."

"I sure hope so."

*Please don't say things you don't mean. And you still owe Liz some flowers. . . .* "Well . . . good night."

She hung up, feeling lost and unhappy and furious with herself. Pausing a moment, she listened, but no sound came from Jake's room. She turned off the lights and went up to bed.

She still couldn't sleep. In a frenzy of thoughts she dozed off and on again, tossing restlessly, kicking off the covers. Strange half-dreams flitted through her mind—black figures wrapped in mysterious capes, trailing blood behind them. A claw groped out for her neck. She shouted and woke herself up.

Groggily Darcy wondered where the sun had gone, then realized it was still night. Her gown was damp with sweat, and as she lay there, a slow chill crawled over her. She turned on her side and heard a soft squeaking sound.

Darcy's eyes went wide, her body tensing in surprise. She couldn't remember the bed squeaking before now, and this strange sound hadn't seemed to come from beneath her. . . .

*Oh, God, it's another rat. . . .*

Bolting upright, her eyes probed the darkness, her ears straining for the scurry of feet across the floor.

Silence.

Darcy pulled the sheets to her chin, afraid to move, afraid to stay where she was. *What if it's crawling up the wall . . . What if it's hiding under the bed—*

*What if it's* in *my bed—*

Choking back a scream, she kicked her legs under the covers, then flapped the sheets around her.

The squeak came again, just above her.

And with it, the soft whirring of wings.

Stunned, Darcy sat there listening, then slowly looked up toward the ceiling.

Something small and black swept quickly out of sight. If she hadn't heard the squeak again, she would have sworn she imagined it.

Holding her breath, Darcy pushed back the covers and got to her knees, her eyes moving slowly over the shadow-speckled ceiling. It reminded her of a spiderweb, all those blurry tendrils of darkness spreading out, oozing into corners she couldn't quite see, so black . . . so still . . .

And then she heard it again.

The soft, soft patter . . . fragile wings flapping . . . beating at the darkness. . . .

The black thing flew straight at her, and as she dived into her pillow, she heard it coming back again, above her bed, its shrill little cry, *Trapped, trapped just like me—*

She grabbed at the lamp, and there were more squeaks—*more wings*—and the hot, still air churning above her head, frantic shadows darting and swooping, trying to find a way out—As her fingers found the light at last, she stared at the ceiling in disbelief.

*Bats.*

Fluttering, falling, fighting for dark places, furry heads and piggy eyes, webbed wings, and *Bats! My God there must be a dozen of them—*

Darcy jumped out of bed and raced downstairs, expecting at any second that the hideous creatures would swoop after her and fill the room like a black cloud.

"Jake!" she shrieked. "Jake—please hurry!"

And as she burst into his room and stared down at his empty bed, she saw that it hadn't even been slept in.

# 14

**B**ats?'' Brandon sounded strange and only half coherent, and for one awful second Darcy was afraid he'd hang up.

"In my room—all *over* my room. Jake's not even here, I don't know where he is—" Her voice broke and struggled for composure. "I was afraid maybe you weren't home."

"I . . . was asleep," he said quietly. "Where do you think I'd be at this hour? Stay downstairs. I'll be right over."

Darcy nodded at the receiver and sat a moment just holding it, as if somehow Brandon's strong voice was still there on the line. She'd closed the door leading up to the attic, but now her eyes fastened on it again, waiting for the soft thud of little bodies on the other side. When nothing happened, she hung up the phone and covered her face with her hands. Where was Jake? A vision of his bloody clothes . . . his bloody hand . . . floated into her mind, and she forced it away. *Oh, Brandon, please hurry.* . . . When she looked up to see him standing in the doorway, she nearly jumped out of her skin.

"God, you scared me to death! How did you get in?"

"I know where Jake hides an extra key." He looked surprised at her outburst. "I thought I'd save you the trouble."

He still looked sleepy, his dark eyes hazy, his hair soft and tousled around his shoulders. He'd thrown on some clothes in a hurry, and his shirt hung unevenly where he'd buttoned it wrong. In spite of everything, Darcy started to smile.

"You look ridiculous," she said.

"Not you," Brandon returned, staring at her. "You look great."

"You *are* still asleep," Darcy scolded, hugging an old bathrobe around her that she'd grabbed from a chair in Jake's room. As Brandon's eyes traveled appreciatively over her body, she flushed and sat down on the couch.

"Please don't look at me," she said.

"Why not?" Brandon grinned. "You're the nicest thing I've seen all day."

Remembering his earlier confrontation with Liz, Darcy firmly changed the subject. "The bats, Brandon. How did they get in? How are we going to get rid of them?"

"Are you all right?" Brandon was still staring, and she nodded. "Honest? You're sure?"

"Yes. Just please get those things out of my room."

"I'll see what I can do." He started up the stairs, paused, and looked back over his shoulder. "You know, if I really *was* Dracula, all I'd have to do is say the word, and they'd obey me and all fly away."

"Then why don't you try it?"

"Okay, here goes."

She heard her bedroom door open, and then his exclamation of disgust. For a moment there was silence, then his voice boomed out, "Be gone!" As she waited expectantly, she heard a flurrying sound, and then his rapid footsteps back down the stairs.

"Well?" She sat forward as he gave a sheepish grin.

"Well . . . they must have known I was an impostor."

"Great. *Now* what are we going to do?"

"I can't figure out how they got in." He frowned. "But maybe—if we can get the screen off—they'll go back outside. I don't suppose you could stir them up a little, could you?"

Darcy's look was reproachful. "I already did that once tonight. What should I do now? Wave my arms and scream? Wave a big towel around?"

Brandon snapped his fingers. "Great idea! I'll get the screen off, and we'll go after them with towels!"

Darcy's eyes narrowed. "You're kidding. Aren't you?"

"Got any better ideas?"

"Well, moving might be a consideration at this point."

"Come on, where's your spirit of adventure? Now, let's see . . . we need some *big* towels—something to put distance between us and them." His voice faded as he disappeared into the bathroom, and she heard him slamming cabinet doors. "Where's Jake keep his towels?"

"You know him better than I do," Darcy mumbled, but she was already heading into Jake's bedroom. "I'll look in here."

The whole thing came back to her as she walked through the door.

In her mind she saw Jake again, covered with blood, tossing something into the closet. *What were you doing, Jake . . . and who was here with you?* She felt frightened even being in the room, and as she opened her mouth to call Brandon, she noticed how the closet door wasn't closed all the way.

Darcy reached out and pulled it open. There was a pile of dirty laundry on the floor, and as she knelt to examine it, she spotted something on the back wall that made her freeze.

It looked like the outline of a door.

Puzzled, Darcy worked the hangers apart and ran her hands over the wall. It felt solid enough, but when she gave it a timid knock, the sound was hollow. *That door on the fire escape?* She'd guessed it might open into Jake's room, and now it looked like she was right—

"Darcy, where'd you go?" Brandon yelled. "Did you find any towels?"

Darcy jumped back guiltily. "Uh . . . I think

so." As she shoved the clothes back in place on the rack, she heard somethng fall with a loud click onto the floor. *Oh, great, something must have fallen from a pocket. . . .*

"Damn!" She could still hear Brandon moving around in the next room, so she leaned down across the laundry pile and fumbled along the floorboards. Just as she was about to give up, her fingers closed around a thin, cylindrical object, and she sat back on her heels, holding it up into the light.

It was a lipstick.

Frowning, Darcy turned it over in her hand, inspecting it closely. It was a cheaper brand, not the kind her mother would have insisted on, and the cap was cracked and dirty. She pulled it off and twirled the base. The lipstick was a garish red and had been worn down almost level with the top of the tube—flat—instead of tapered at one side.

"Darcy?"

Flustered, Darcy tossed the lipstick back into the closet and jumped up.

"Oh, there you are—hey, I found these in the kitchen." Brandon started for the stairs and motioned her to follow. "You know, I've been thinking, maybe it's not such a good idea, you going up there again. Once I get that window open, I can probably handle it myself." He threw her a sly glance. "So *what* if I get bitten? So *what* if I die of rabies?"

"Oh, please"—Darcy gave him a push from behind—"spare me the martyrdom. I wouldn't dream of sending you in there alone."

"Wow. What courage. What fortitude. What—"

"Lunacy. The two of us and a room full of bats."

They stood together, eyeing her bedroom door.

"Or I could do the really sensible thing," Brandon mused.

"What's that?"

"Call Kyle in the morning and have *him* help me."

"That *is* a sensible thing." Darcy nodded. "Are you hungry?"

"Always." Brandon followed her back to the kitchen and slouched into a chair as she rummaged through the refrigerator. "Okay, let me guess. No food."

"Doesn't he ever eat?" Darcy shook her head. "I don't think I've ever seen him eat since I've been here. What does he live on anyway?" She let the door swing shut, then stood a moment, staring at nothing, debating whether or not to tell Brandon what she'd witnessed in Jake's room that evening. *Maybe it's nothing. . . . I shouldn't jump to conclusions . . . just because I don't understand. . . .* Aloud she said, "I wasn't even thinking straight once I saw those bats, Brandon. I shouldn't have called you."

"Sure you should have."

"No, I feel really silly now for having done that. It was nice of you to come over, but you don't have to stay."

He did his best to look crestfallen. "You mean I'm dismissed? Just like that?"

She smiled. "Free to go."

"Hmmm . . ." He pretended to be deep in thought, and then a lazy grin crept across his face.

"I don't think I want to go. So now you're stuck with me." His eyes traveled over her again, his grin widening as she blushed.

"Brandon . . . stop doing that. . . ."

"Stop doing what?" he asked innocently. "My eyes are tired. When my eyes are tired, I can't control them. They just look where they want to look." He reached out and caught her around the waist, his expression sobering. "You sounded really scared when you called tonight. Are you sure it was just the bats?"

Darcy's glance was quick. "Why do you say that?"

He was quiet for a long minute as his dark eyes searched hers. "Just a feeling, I guess," he said quietly and pulled her toward him. "It's not easy being the new kid."

"No"—she tried to smile—"but it's not just that.'

"What, then?"

She gestured vaguely toward the ceiling. "Why would someone put bats in my room? And leave a dead rat in my bed?"

She felt him tensing beneath his calm exterior. "You think someone . . . *did* that? On purpose?"

"Well, they're not things that just *happen* to people, are they?" Darcy sounded defensive. "Not just your usual run-of-the-mill coincidences?"

"But . . . why?" He looked genuinely astonished, and she pulled away.

"You sound like Kyle. That's just what Kyle said when I told him about Elliott."

"What about Elliott?"

"I keep seeing him. In crowds, I mean. Watching me."

Brandon stared at her. "Elliott. Watching you."

"Oh, forget it," Darcy grumbled. "I never should have said anything."

"Yes, you should." Brandon reached out again, but she turned neatly out of his reach. "You should tell me whatever's bothering you—"

"And who are you? Dr. Dracula, the famous psychologist?"

"Hey, Darcy, come on, if you're upset about something—"

"I'm upset about a lot of things." Her chin lifted stubbornly. "Like Jake, for starters. He calls those monsters downstairs his *family,* for God's sake. And tonight he said he was going to bed, and he's not even here."

"Well, so Jake's a little unusual."

"Unusual?" Darcy gaped at him. *"Unusual?" Now . . . I'll tell him now—*

"Calm down, will you? You're getting upset over nothing."

"Yes, I'm upset. I think someone's trying to hurt me."

"Hurt you?" Brandon grew quiet, his eyes lifting in a sidelong glance. "Who'd want to hurt you, Darcy? Besides Liz, I mean."

He said it so matter-of-factly that Darcy's retort died on her lips. As she locked eyes with Brandon, she saw the uneasy look on his face, and then his eyes lowered to the tabletop between them.

"I know she does," Darcy said then, barely a whisper. "I think you'd better go." She went into the living room and sat down stiffly at one end of the couch. She picked up the remote control and turned on the TV, then stared at the screen as a black and white movie came into focus. On the screen a woman ran for her life through a foggy forest. From the fog came the howl of a wolf . . . and from the kitchen behind Darcy came the soft approach of footsteps. Darcy kept her eyes on the movie, and Brandon sat down beside her.

"You've got to understand Liz." He sighed, and Darcy shook her head.

"I think I've gone above and beyond understanding—"

"You have. I swear you have." His hands went up in a gesture of defeat. "Liz is the center of her own universe, and she expects to be the center of everyone else's. See, even at home it's always been Liz is the smartest and Liz has all the potential and Liz has all the promise and the sun rises and sets on Liz. I mean, poor Kyle . . . he's the rebellious one 'cause he rides a motorcycle and wants to be a musician. *He* never gives them any trouble, but he's the disappointment and Liz is the star. Liz gets anything she wants. Liz deserves the best. So how could she be any different than the way she is?" He shook his head slowly. "And when Liz gets stood up to . . . or disappointed . . . the gods get very angry." He stole a look at her, and she began to smile.

"You're so accepting of everyone, aren't you? You and Kyle both. Of Jake . . . of Elliott . . . you're not judgmental like so many people are. Like I am."

He shook his head at her. "Are you kidding? Kyle maybe, but not me. I mean, half the time I'm ready to kill Liz, she drives me so crazy." He thought a moment. "What I'm trying to say is, I understand the way she is, but that doesn't make it okay."

"I don't know why I'm letting her upset me so much. I'll just have to be better about it."

"Hey, don't be so hard on yourself. Liz has it out for you, no doubt about that. And that's probably my fault."

"But Jake gave me her job—"

"But I," Brandon began, then looked away, his voice uncomfortable. "I mean . . . *I* . . . thought you were pretty great when I first saw your picture."

"My picture?"

"Yeah, Jake showed us all your picture before you got here. I guess your mom sent it in a letter sometime to your aunt."

"I didn't know that."

"I guess he wasn't exactly thrilled about you coming. He really didn't know what he was in for."

"I can imagine."

"Hey, don't let Jake get you down. I don't think he's had much love in his life. I've never heard him mention a relationship in a positive way. I don't think he can handle feelings very well."

Darcy just looked at him, guilt and confusion flooding through her.

"Yeah, Jake's all right," Brandon mumbled. He gazed at the TV screen where a vampire was unfolding himself from a long, black cape. "And . . . you know . . . *I* care about you, Darcy. And Liz knows it."

For a moment the only sound was from the television . . . impassioned breathing as the vampire leaned closer . . . closer . . . to the woman's throat. . . .

Darcy felt Brandon beside her . . . his soft warm breath caressing her ear . . . her neck. . . .

She closed her eyes and lost herself in his kiss.

# 15

The first thing Darcy saw when she woke up was Brandon's shoulder beneath her cheek. They were still sitting on the couch, propped against each other where they'd fallen asleep talking, and daylight was streaming through the window.

The second thing she saw was Liz standing in the doorway.

In that split second Darcy thought she knew what it must feel like to get struck by lightning. She bolted upright, excuses spinning through her brain, and Brandon toppled over on his face, mumbling into the cushions. At that instant Jake wandered out of the kitchen and nodded in Darcy's general direction.

"I can handle surprises," he said, deadpan. "Like never knowing what I might find when I come home. . . ."

Darcy had the eerie sensation of being trapped in a horror scene just like one of the statues in the Dungeon. A sign flashed through her mind: SUMMER VISITOR TORN TO PIECES BY VICIOUS REDHEAD. Jake stopped in his tracks and flashed a guileless smile at the door. He looked like he was enjoying himself immensely.

"Why, Liz—I didn't hear you knock."

As Brandon's eyes fluttered open, bringing the whole room into focus, he turned his head into the pillows and groaned.

"Oh, no. . . ."

Liz looked positively livid. Darcy had never seen the girl's face such a perfect match for her hair. As Liz's eyes burned into her, Darcy mumbled the first thing that came into her mind.

"Bats," she said, and some remote part of her brain couldn't believe how stupid that sounded. "He just came over to get the bats out of my room."

"Bats," Jake echoed, going back into the kitchen. "Now, that's one I haven't heard."

"It's true!" Darcy blurted out. "Bats—*everywhere!*" To her horror she saw Kyle's head appear over Liz's shoulder and a slow grin spread over his face.

" 'Morning, Darcy. 'Morning, Bran." Kyle said, and Brandon groaned again.

"Hey, man, this isn't what you're thinking—"

"How do *you* know what I'm thinking?" Kyle's grin vanished instantly as Liz whirled on him. It made Darcy think he'd had a lot of practice at it.

"You shut up," Liz ordered Kyle. "And *you*"— her withering glance fell on Brandon, who peered out around one pillow—"you *will* still take me to the concert tonight as promised. And you *will* have a lot of explaining to do."

The whole apartment shook as she slammed the door behind her, and Kyle just managed to side-step into the room before he was crushed. He threw Brandon a sympathetic look.

"Isn't that just like her? Most girls try to punish you by *depriving* you of their company."

"Well"—Jake leaned in the doorway and raised his coffee cup with a bitter smile—"here's to sisters and their sensitivity."

Darcy stared at his other hand, which was half hidden behind his back and wrapped in bandages. For the first time she noticed how really pale he looked.

"What happened to your hand?" she murmured.

"I hurt it." He met her stare, unflinching, and downed his coffee in one gulp.

"And you just got home? Where were you?" She tried to sound concerned, not suspicious, but Jake turned away.

"A little problem at the Club—someone got careless with matches."

"Jake—a fire? Is it—"

"Okay," he said, cutting off the boys' questions before they could even ask them. "Hardly any damage. Nothing to worry about. We're open for business as usual."

"Not to change the subject"—Brandon rolled over and flung one arm across his eyes—"but there *are* bats in Darcy's room. We've got to get them out of there."

"All you have to do is pick them up," Kyle said. "It's daylight; they'll just hang there and sleep."

"And since when are you such an expert on bats?" Brandon grumbled.

"Since I helped you with all your vampire research, remember?" Kyle made a face at Darcy. "Just like a celebrity—how quickly he forgets."

"Brandon, that's so easy." Darcy looked at him accusingly. "Why didn't you think of that? Then you wouldn't have had to come over last night—"

"One guess," Kyle intimated, and Brandon shot him a look as he stretched and yawned.

"Well, I'm not picking them up by myself. And we still have to turn them loose somewhere."

"How about the park?" Kyle suggested, looking at Jake.

"Sure. Whatever." Jake shrugged as if bats in his house was the most natural occurrence in the world, and Darcy watched the three of them troop upstairs. In no time at all the room was declared officially exorcised, and she hurried up to dress.

"It's still early," Brandon said when she came back down. "You don't open till ten, and I'm starving. Is anyone in the mood for breakfast besides me?"

"Tell you what," Darcy offered, "if we can get some eggs and vegetables, I'll fix omelettes."

"I need something with iron." Brandon struck a vampirish pose. "Remember my delicate digestion—"

"We can go to the Farmer's Market," Kyle said. "They'll probably have everything we need. You coming, Jake?"

"No, I'm not hungry. I've got to get over to the Club."

"Oh, come on," Kyle protested. "You know what they say—all work and no play—it'll be good for you."

"No. I don't want to go."

Brandon swung an arm around Jake's neck, locking the two of them side by side down the stairs. "We won't take no for an answer. You need the fresh air . . . the exercise . . ."

"The crazy people," Jake retorted. "Every crazy in the city shows up at the market on Saturday morning." He looked from Brandon to Kyle. "I rest my case."

"Come on, it'll be fun," Brandon coaxed, his grip tightening as Jake tried to pull away.

"I mean it, you guys, I've got to get to work—"

"Time to work is later," Kyle said, smiling. "Time to play is now."

As Brandon and Kyle urged Jake down the sidewalk, Darcy couldn't help noticing how tense and withdrawn Jake seemed. His eyes kept scanning the crowds as if looking for someone, yet she had the uneasy feeling that he didn't want to be seen. When they reached the market and merged with the noisy Saturday shoppers, Kyle waited for her while the others went on.

"Don't want to lose you." He winked, and she smiled back.

"You won't."

"You never know. Liz might be hiding somewhere." He gave her that contagious grin and added, "She might be disguised."

Brandon caught that last remark and spun around.

"Wait—that looks like a very sweet lady over there—oh, *no! It's Liz in disguise!*"

They laughed uproariously over the joke, but Jake didn't join in. He was checking his watch and then the crowd, and his expression looked strained.

"Jake, I think you should move Darcy downstairs," Brandon said, but when Jake didn't answer, he got louder. "I said you should move Darcy—"

"I heard you," Jake said impatiently.

"And you move to the attic."

"Okay. Sure. Whatever she wants."

"You're lucky she'll even stay in that apartment after what happened," Brandon went on. "All those bats—"

"I don't know why you're making such a big deal out of those damn bats—"

"Big deal—" Darcy began, but Jake cut her off.

"—when they probably just came in from the crawl space."

"What crawl space?" Brandon, Kyle, and Darcy echoed in unison.

Jake looked at them as if they were slow-witted children. "There's a little space in the wall down near the floor. It's practically under the bed. I keep boxes and stuff stored in there."

"Stuff?" Brandon snorted. "You mean, like bats? That kind of stuff?"

"Oh, sure, Brandon," Jake came back at him. "I *breed* them. It's one of my *side* jobs."

"Oh, God"—Darcy shuddered—"they could have been crawling all over me—"

"They probably nested in there and just wanted a change of scenery." Jake shrugged. "I mean, it's not like anything happened, right? They're just bats!"

"Well, what if they didn't come from the crawl space?" Darcy blurted out. "What if they came from somewhere else?" Three pairs of eyes fastened on her, and she lowered her voice. "What I mean is . . . where *else* could they have come from?"

Jake looked impatient. "How should I know? A cave, maybe. Some old abandoned building."

"There aren't any caves around here," Kyle chuckled.

"Then I give up. You tell *me* where they came from." Jake's nervous glance went over their surroundings and he walked on ahead of them.

"What's his problem?" Kyle mumbled.

"Who knows?" Brandon shook his head. "But he sure doesn't act like he wants to be here."

"What really happened to his hand?"

Brandon shrugged. "Well, *I'm* not going to ask him."

"Me, neither."

As Kyle and Brandon made their way along a row of stalls, Darcy caught up with Jake.

"You seem kind of nervous," she said casually, choosing some avocados and tomatoes. "Didn't you sleep well?"

"No." He gave his head an abrupt shake. "Are we through here? Can we go? I've got a million things to do."

"Well, why don't you go, then?" Darcy frowned as Jake walked away and Kyle rejoined her. "What's *wrong* with him any—" As her gaze followed Jake's retreat, she suddenly grabbed Kyle's arm. "There's Elliott."

"What? Where?"

"There!" She shoved her purchases at him and began to run.

"Darcy!" Kyle stood helplessly, watching her go in one direction, Brandon in another. "Hey! What are you—*wait!* Wait a minute!" Dropping his things, he started after her, but with her head start, he quickly lost sight of her in the crowd.

"Elliott!" Darcy knew she hadn't imagined it this time, his thin pale face staring out at her from the throngs of busy shoppers—and as she tried to maneuver through the crowd, her fear turned to anger. "Stop, Elliott! *Stop!*" She saw several curious heads turn and began to shout louder. "Stop that guy! He stole my purse!" To her annoyance, no one joined in the chase, and she gritted her teeth and ran harder.

He was unbelievably fast. If Darcy hadn't known better, she would have sworn he was flying. She swung around the corner of a fruit stand and stopped, groaning in frustration. She was behind the marketplace now, facing a weed-grown lot and broken and abandoned stalls. Nothing moved except a few pieces of windblown paper and a stray dog.

*"Damn!"* She plopped down on one of the dilapidated counters, trying to catch her breath. She felt sick from the heat and not eating. And as she drew deep gulps of air into her lungs, she had the sudden feeling that she wasn't alone.

Again she scanned the deserted lot, her uneasiness growing. *Why did I run off like that? No one even knows where I am. . . .*

She looked down at her feet, down at the broken concrete. It was smeared with something red.

A pair of sunglasses was lying on the ground.

"Elliott," she whispered.

As Darcy leaned forward, a hand shot out from underneath the boarded-up counter and wrapped tightly around her ankle. She screamed and tried to jerk her foot away, but it only slid a few inches, trapped in someone's wet grasp.

"Help me! Somebody! Help!" She felt herself being dragged slowly down, and she struggled harder. Grabbing up a piece of wood, she swung it back blindly, then heard an unexpected thud as something hit the ground behind her.

"Jake! Oh, *no*—did I hurt you? Are you all right?"

She didn't even realize she was free again until she fell on her knees beside him, horrified at what she'd done. "Oh, Jake—I didn't mean to! I thought—"

Jake lay there, too stunned to move. After several minutes he swore under his breath and got unsteadily to his feet. He was covered with mud. As he brushed angrily at his clothes, Darcy pointed to the stand.

"Elliott—" she said breathlessly, "hurry—he's under here—"

Jake was still glaring at her, still smearing mud up and down his sleeves.

"Elliott!" Darcy said again. "What's the matter with you! Didn't you hear what I—"

"What's the matter with *me!*" Jake gave her an

incredulous look. "What's the matter with *you?* You nearly knocked my goddamn head off!"

"Don't you understand?" Darcy grabbed him and pointed. "Look—there's his—" Her mouth fell open and she stared.

The glasses were gone.

"No. I don't believe this." Darcy fell on her knees beside the counter and tried to peer in through the broken slats.

"What do you think you're *doing?*" Jake's tolerance was at the breaking point, but Darcy was determined to crawl through the tiny opening.

"I'm looking for— He's not here!"

"And you're surprised? You're talking about him like he's some kind of slug or something—"

"It was Elliott!" Darcy scrambled up again, her face flexing between anger and tears as she surveyed the rest of the booth. "He must have crawled out the back! But he was *here!* I saw him in the crowd, and I chased him—look at my foot!" She stuck out her leg, her eyes widening at the dark red streaks on her shoe and ankle. "It's blood! See that?"

"Yeah, well, so is this." Jake wiped at the messy cut on his head. "That's what happens when you get your skull cracked open with a two-by-four."

She stared at him, but he shifted his eyes away and attacked his muddy jeans with a vengeance. "I'm sorry I hurt you," she said quietly. "But do you really think I'd make something like this up?"

"Come on, let's just go back."

"Why did you follow me?" Darcy asked, but

Jake continued brushing himself off. "Why did you come after me?"

Jake's quick movements slowed . . . stopped. For a long moment he studied the mud on his shoes. "Kyle said you'd run off. I . . . got worried."

"You and Brandon weren't even around Kyle. How did you know where I'd gone?"

Jake's stare was as even as her own. "Kyle started yelling—and I saw you run off. I heard all the commotion—you were parting the crowd like the Red Sea. You don't have to be a damn detective to—"

"Was there really a fire at the Club last night?" Darcy blurted out. "You said you were going to bed, but you weren't even there when Brandon came over—"

"What—I have to check *in* with you?" Jake gave a derisive snort, but his hands were busy again, brushing at his shirt with quick, nervous gestures.

"Someone put a rat in my bed and bats in my room and Elliott's been following me—"

"And I'm supposed to know about all that?" he returned impatiently. "Sounds like just a bunch of coincidences to me. You can't go around accusing Elliott of something you're not even sure of. Come on, let's get out of here—"

"Why are you so *nervous?*" Darcy's voice raised. "Why do you keep looking around like that? Are we being watched? Are you scared of something—"

"Hey, I just don't want to be here, okay? All this talk about rats and bats and people stalking you—you're making me crazy! Now, will you just lay off?'' For a split second he sounded almost threatening. "Don't nag me, Darcy—I don't like it. And I don't like girls who do it. You're starting to sound just like your mother—"

"Don't you *say* that! Don't you ever say that to me!'' Without warning Darcy flew at him, only this time when he hit the ground, he took Darcy with him. As she tried to swing at him, he pinned her arms easily, looking down at her from his vantage point on top.

"What do you think—"

"Get *off* me!'' Darcy was furious, but the more she struggled, the tighter he held her. "What kind of an uncle are you anyway? Beating up on your own niece—"

"Quit calling me your uncle!'' Jake slammed her arms down hard and glared at her. "I'm *not* your uncle! We're not even *related!*''

His face was just inches from hers. As Darcy gazed at him open-mouthed, the sparks in his green eyes began to fade.

"I'm adopted. And I bet your mom and dear Aunt Alicia never told you *that,* did they? Hell, no—it would have offended their sense of—of *propriety*—and—and—good *breeding!* As if that wasn't bad enough already, I lived with their *father*—who they *hated* because he was a plain, decent man who couldn't have cared less about *money!*''

Darcy felt his heart hammering against hers. Without warning he rolled off and released her.

"Forget it,'' he grumbled. "Get up.''

They started back without a word, Jake avoiding Darcy's confused eyes. As they slowly approached the street, Kyle ran up to them, out of breath.

"Where were you?" His hands went nervously through his hair. "We looked everywhere—"

"Yeah, so what's up?" Jake cut him off.

Kyle didn't seem to notice their disheveled appearances as he glanced anxiously toward the market. "I can't believe it—this is awful—they found somebody—"

For the first time now Darcy began to notice the commotion, people running, gathering at one end of the stands. She could hear muffled screams and faraway shouting. In the distance a police siren wailed.

"What is it?" She could feel the fear in the air, and she heard Kyle's answer even before he spoke—

"A girl," he said, and he sounded numb and sad and horrified all at once. "The Vampire—her—her throat—"

And as Darcy stared down at her foot, she could almost feel the wet hand leaving its bloodprint on her ankle.

# 16

"Why are you two acting so surprised?" Darcy looked from Brandon to Kyle and then back again. Jake had gone on to the Club, and now they were almost to the apartment, yet neither of the boys had hardly said a word. "Why is it so hard for you to believe?" She saw a look pass between them, and her voice grew more insistent. "I'm *not* imagining this!"

"We didn't say that," Brandon said quickly.

"You're *thinking* it—"

"I didn't think it." Kyle shook his head adamantly. "Brandon didn't think it, and I didn't think it."

"Okay." Brandon draped an arm across Darcy's shoulders as they stopped in front of the Dungeon. "We'll just ask him."

"Great idea!" Kyle brightened.

"You'll just ask him." Darcy folded her arms across her chest and gave the two of them a scathing look. "And of course he'll just *admit* that he's been following me." Again the look passed between them. "I have to *work* with this guy, remember? *Alone!*"

"Well . . ." Brandon shrugged and glanced at Kyle. "I mean, what do you want us to say? Elliott's an okay guy—"

"Oh, right. He had blood all over his hand, and then some poor girl was found with her throat cut open." She gave an exasperated groan. "Why won't you listen to me?"

"We're listening." Kyle nodded.

"Yeah, but I can't believe what we're hearing." Brandon studied Darcy's stubborn face. "You're serious, aren't you? About that hand . . . and what happened to that girl at the market. What kind of an accusation is *that?* How do you even know it was Elliott's hand?"

Darcy didn't hesitate. "I saw his sunglasses on the ground. He must have dropped them."

"Oh, well, that proves it, then!" Brandon threw up his hands in mock defeat. "Come on, Darcy, Elliott wouldn't hurt a fly. He might be a little strange, but—"

"A *little* strange?"

"But he's . . ." Kyle stammered, searching for words. "You know, kind to kids and animals and—"

"What's wrong with you two?" Darcy narrowed her eyes. "You act like you're hiding something." And for the third time a secretive sort of look passed between the boys.

Darcy made breakfast, but all the fun had gone out of the occasion. She felt strangely removed from Brandon and Kyle's conversation, her mind going relentlessly over all the strange events that had taken place in the past few days. She dreaded being with Elliott at work today, but when she finally went downstairs to open up, he was already letting customers in. She welcomed the steady stream of visitors—it gave her an excuse to avoid him. When closing time came, he escaped while she chatted with a customer, and she was glad to get upstairs and change for the concert.

She hadn't been able to stop thinking about Jake all day.

As Darcy wandered restlessly through the apartment, her thoughts kept going back to the Farmer's Market and what had happened there that morning. *How did Jake know where I was—why was he so nervous?* Again she heard the desperate voice in his bedroom—*"I can't stand this anymore. . . ."*

"What is it, Jake?" she whispered now. "What's making me feel so afraid?" She remembered the confession he'd made at the market, and the expression on his face as he'd looked down at her, and a whole range of confused emotions went through her. *"I'm not your uncle . . . we're not even related."*

She realized she was standing in his room, staring at his closet. The door was half open, dirty clothes spilling out onto the floor. She opened it and stared down at the pile. *You threw something in here last night . . . what was it?*

She reached down and picked up a towel, wondering how it could have gotten so muddy, all those dark stains . . . mostly dried now and stiff to the touch. . . . Only now she could see they weren't really brown at all, but more of a reddish color, like old rust, and not a muddy smell, but another, stranger kind of odor. . . .

"Get out of there, Darcy," Jake said, and she whirled around, flinging the towel guiltily onto the floor.

"You . . . you scared me." She fought for composure. "I didn't hear you come home. . . ."

Jake walked slowly over to where she was standing. He reached past her and closed the closet door.

"What were you looking for?" he asked, and his voice was smooth and very, very calm.

She realized he hadn't seen what she'd been holding, and she blurted out the first thing she could think of.

"I thought you might have an umbrella I could use—it looks rainy again, and there's that concert tonight. Are you going?"

"No." He stood there, eyes going to the ceiling . . . down the wall . . . across the floor. For a moment he looked as if he was going to say something, then seemed to change his mind. He started out the door . . . stopped . . . looked back at her. Darcy moved past him into the living room.

"Don't ever go in my room again," Jake said.

"No." Darcy shook her head, her voice barely a whisper. "I won't. I'm sorry."

She didn't realize how badly she was shaking until Jake was gone again. Nausea rushed over her, and she sagged against the wall. *Blood . . . the towel all soaked and stained, oh, God.* . . . She forced a deep breath into her lungs and tried to think logically. *It could be anything, really, lots of things could stain that color, but what did you do to your hand, Jake, and "I didn't expect it . . . the struggle. . . ."*

She thought of the body she'd found in the alley . . . and the body discovered just hours ago in the market.

"What did they see before they died?" Darcy whispered. *"Who* did they see?"

"Darcy?"

She jumped back, swallowing a scream. "God, Kyle, I didn't hear you come in."

"Sorry. I knocked, but nobody answered." He motioned toward the stairs. "You ready? I came by the park on my way, and the band's already warming up."

"Great. Let's get out of here."

It felt good to be out in the fresh air where she could breathe . . . where she could think. On the back of Kyle's motorcycle she closed her eyes and tilted her face into the wind, loving the sting of it against her cheeks, something natural and real. And then, as Kyle rolled to a stop in the parking lot, she suddenly buried her face against his back.

"Hey." Kyle twisted around, concerned. "What's wrong?"

She forced a smile, shaking her head. For a minute she didn't trust herself to speak.

"Darcy?"

"It's just . . ." She bit her lip and forced a laugh. "It's nothing. I'm just feeling . . . I don't know . . . empty or something."

He didn't laugh. His eyes searched hers, and

in their depths she recognized real understanding. "Hey," he said and reached out to give her an awkward pat, "hey, it's . . . you know . . . going to be okay."

*Is it, Kyle? I want to believe you . . . but is something really wrong here, or am I just being paranoid?*

"We don't have to do this," Kyle was saying, his eyes full of worry. "I can take you back, or we can go anywhere you like."

"No," Darcy said firmly. "That's sweet, but no. I'm not going to ruin your evening."

"You're not." He smiled. "Quit talking like that."

"I'm being difficult. I do that sometimes."

"Uh-oh. Then maybe you need a spanking." Kyle's eyes twinkled as he helped her off. "It's a tempting thought, but Brandon probably wouldn't be too happy about it."

"Now *you* quit talking like that." Darcy blushed. "There's nothing going on between Brandon and me, and he's in enough trouble already."

"Nothing, huh?" Kyle gave her a sly look. "That's not what *I* hear."

"What do you mean? What do *you* hear?"

"My, my, but we seem awfully curious." Kyle laughed, walking a little ahead. "But I should warn you, Liz isn't going to give him up without a fight."

"You're pretty presumptuous." Darcy looked indignant, but Kyle only chuckled.

"Presumptuous?" he teased. "Just because Brandon woke up on your couch this morning?"

"I told you before, we were just talking and we fell asleep," Darcy sighed, exasperated. "Anyway, he's probably the kind who attracts girls like crazy." She tried to sound indifferent, but Kyle stole a knowing glance at her.

"He's the best," Kyle agreed. "At just about everything." Then with a wink, "But you're different, aren't you?"

"Different how?"

"From all his others."

"All his others, huh?"

Kyle gave another grin, then led the way to the outdoor stage. The viewing area was already packed. As they found a spot near the front, Kyle stood a moment, looking around.

"Brandon's supposed to meet us here. If Liz doesn't kill him first."

Darcy didn't find the subject that amusing. As she sat down on the ground, she noticed Kyle watching her thoughtfully.

"Darcy . . . I have to tell you something."

"Then come down here." She patted the grass beside her and wondered why he suddenly seemed so ill at ease. For a moment he stared off into the distance, then slowly sank down beside her.

"You're not going to like it," he said quietly.

Her face changed from surprise to suspicion. "Kyle . . . what's this all about?"

Again he hesitated. His eyes lowered guiltily.

"Kyle—"

"The rat," he mumbled. And then, as if afraid of losing his nerve, he blurted, "We put it there. In your bed, I mean." He looked away from her, and Darcy regarded him speechlessly.

"You . . . did . . . what?"

"It was just—you know"—he gestured vaguely—

"it was . . ." Finally his eyes met hers. "Not very funny," he finished lamely.

Darcy stared him down. "No. No, it wasn't very funny."

"Liz was mad about your getting her job," he said, talking to the ground, resting his chin on one knee. "Jake told her that night at the Club right as we were leaving. And she was already jealous of you because of your picture."

"The one Jake got from Aunt Alicia?

He nodded. "When Jake showed it to us, Brandon thought you were really beautiful—only he made the mistake of saying it out loud in front of Liz."

"So the rat was really her idea."

Another reluctant nod. "When she told me about it, I didn't want any part of it—"

"So why did you do it?" Darcy nudged him with her foot, but he wouldn't look at her.

"She said she'd tell Jake that Brandon and I smuggled beer into the Club one night—I mean, we didn't even drink it, it was just a dare, but if Jake ever found out, that'd be the end of my job. He wouldn't even let me in the building. He doesn't put up with stuff like that." He thought a minute and gave a wry smile. "I don't even know why I'm worried about it anymore—it looks like I'll be losing my job anyway."

Darcy shook her head angrily. "What about Jake and that dumb story about his cat?"

"He told me he told you that so you wouldn't think some psycho was after you."

"Does he know *you* did it?"

Kyle squirmed uncomfortably. "He figured Liz

did it. He told me he thought it was her, but he wasn't going to give her the satisfaction of making a big deal out of it. He said . . . well . . . that you were really upset.''

"That's putting it mildly. So what else have you done?''

"Nothing.'' Kyle sighed and buried his face in his arms. "I feel terrible.''

"You should.'' Darcy got up and brushed herself off while Kyle mumbled into his knees.

"Where you going?''

"I don't know,'' Darcy said irritably. "I'm just going.''

Kyle took the hint he wasn't welcome and stayed put as Darcy set off through the trees. She wasn't sure how she felt anymore—hurt, angry, or even amused at Liz's immaturity. Of course Brandon would have known about it, too. . . . She hated being the butt of a joke when everyone was in on it but her. As she followed a path through the park, she even considered running away—just finding a phone and calling a cab and going straight to the bus station. She didn't know what to think about *anyone* anymore. *I'm just the outsider. As usual.*

She stopped at a fountain and splashed cool water over her face, pressing her hands to her eyes, trying to put her thoughts into proper perspective. A screen of trees enclosed the spot where she stood, but just beyond the greenery a couple was engaged in an argument. Darcy tried to ignore their heated words until she realized the voices were familiar.

"Why is *this* one so special?'' Liz snapped.

"What is it about *this* one that's got your charm working overtime?"

"She happens to be a very nice girl," Brandon retorted angrily. "Which, I might add, is a pleasant change."

"Yeah? Well, I know she'll end up like all the others you go after. I know you'll try to make me jealous, and then you'll dump her and come back to me. Just like always."

"You're really sick, Liz, you know that?" Brandon sounded tired. "Really *sick*."

As Darcy glanced up, she saw Kyle standing beside her, his face like a scolded puppy.

"I know you're really upset, and I don't blame you, but you shouldn't be wandering around alone out—" He broke off in surprise as he heard Liz lash into a tirade, and then he gently touched Darcy's shoulder. "Come on, you don't want to hear this."

"You really think you're perfect, don't you?" Liz's fury carried loud and clear, and Kyle winced. "God's gift to women? Well, let me tell me something, Mister Tall, Dark, and Stupid, if you don't stay away from little Miss Darcy, I *promise* you I'll fix it—*personally*—so *no* one will even want to *look* at her again!"

"Shut up, Liz, just—shut—up—"

"I mean it, Brandon, I swear if you don't forget about her, I'll—"

And suddenly she choked, as if her body had been jolted, as if her threat had been stopped half-way in her throat. In their hiding place Kyle looked at Darcy and slowly squeezed her hand.

"And you listen to me." Brandon ·spoke carefully . . . deliberately . . . every syllable tight and controlled. "If you dare—if you even *think* about doing *anything* to Darcy . . . I swear—"

"You'll do what?" Liz said smugly.

Silence fell, thick and dangerous.

As Darcy rested her head against Kyle's shoulder, they heard Brandon's heels fading swiftly into the night.

# 17

**P**lease, Darcy, I wish you'd forget about it,"
Kyle said for the tenth time. "They argue like that
all the time. You wouldn't believe some of their
fights."

Darcy nodded wearily. "I bet I would." She
unlocked the lobby door, then turned and looked
up into his face. "I enjoyed the concert."

"Liar."

"Well, I *tried* to enjoy the concert. And thanks
for being honest about the rat. That took a lot of
guts."

Kyle let out a low whistle. "Yeah, it sure did."
As Darcy smiled at him, his eyes crinkled up into
a relieved grin. "No more worrying, okay? I
mean, I *live* with her; I'll keep an eye on her all
night."

She knew he was trying to make a joke, but she

didn't feel like laughing. As he walked back to his motorcycle, she stopped him.

"Kyle . . . I'm really sorry about the problems in your band. Can't you find another one that needs a drummer? I think you're so good. I've never been able to figure out how drummers can do ten things at the same time."

"Quick hands." He chuckled modestly. "This city's full of good drummers. But maybe . . . yeah . . . I might be able to find another group to play with. Jake said he'd keep his ears open."

"Speaking of Jake, can I ask you something else?"

"Anything."

"Why isn't he ever home at night? What does he do?"

Kyle paused, digging his keys from his pocket. "Well, he's in charge of the whole place, and the owner's never there, so I guess he does everything."

"Are you *sure* that's where he is every night?"

"Well, sure." Kyle shrugged. "Where else would he be?"

Darcy watched him leave, then went up to her room. It didn't take long to inspect for bats, but even though everything seemed normal, she still felt uneasy. *So what else have you been up to, Liz? Things that haven't even happened yet?*

She slept fitfully, her dreams full of black-caped strangers with Jake's green eyes and Brandon's deep voice. A shadowy whisperer tempted and threatened her, and when she begged him to reveal himself, she saw Elliott without his glasses and empty sockets where his eyes should have been.

She dreamed she was in terrible danger.

She dreamed someone was in her room.

In one terrorized second she woke up, realizing that this was no dream. And as a childhood instinct took over, she lay perfectly, silently still.

The figure stood at the foot of her bed. She could feel invisible eyes watching her . . . inspecting her. . . .

He glided noiselessly to her pillow.

Darcy felt every nerve contract, and her body turned to ice. She could hear her rapid breathing . . . could feel her heart thumping out of control.

A faint warm breath trailed across her neck. In one swift flash of insight Darcy wondered how it would feel to have her throat slit.

"Darcy," a voice whispered.

From downstairs a door slammed.

Immediately Darcy sensed a change in her intruder, *sensed* rather than saw, felt his sudden tension, his hand paralyzed upon her hair, the faint stir of air as he slid away from the bed. She heard her bedroom door closing softly . . . the muffled footsteps down the stairs. And then . . . voices . . . familiar voices . . . but low and urgent, as if they didn't want to be heard.

"What are you doing here?" And that was Jake's voice, Darcy knew it at once as she pressed her ear to the door. "Do you know how late it is?"

"We just thought you should know," Brandon said. "Liz threatened Darcy tonight."

"So what? Liz is always threatening someone."

"No, this was different." Kyle's voice, tense and unhappy. "I think she really means it."

"I do, too," Brandon echoed.

"And let me guess what brought this on," Jake said sarcastically. "You and your overactive hormones?"

"That's not fair." Brandon's voice raised. "I really like Darcy!"

"You like everything that's female—"

"Come on," Kyle broke in, "let's think about Darcy. She might be in danger or something."

Jake sighed. "So how do you know about all this?" The couch groaned several times as if they'd all sat down.

"We were at the concert," Kyle said, "and Darcy went off by herself and—Brandon and Liz were fighting—"

"Great timing," Brandon grumbled. "I guess she heard it all."

"I guess," Kyle said softly. "I tried to play it down. I don't want her getting all paranoid. Even if she should be," he added reluctantly.

"Someone's going to have to keep an eye on Liz," Brandon said.

"She's *your* girl, *you* keep an eye on her—"

"Well, she's *your* sister."

"So what?"

"Will you two cut it out?" Darcy could picture Jake throwing up his hands in his standard gesture of impatience. "When are you guys going to learn that Liz is ninety-nine percent bluff?"

For a long moment there was silence. Then finally Kyle mumbled, "Well, we thought you should know."

"Fine. Thanks. Now go home. Nothing's going to happen to Darcy."

"Unless," Brandon spoke up, "Liz decides to use that other one percent."

"*Nothing* is going to happen to Darcy," Jake said again emphatically. "Liz isn't going to touch her."

Darcy heard the door close . . . the sudden silence.

"No one is going to touch Darcy," Jake said aloud to the empty room. "I'll see to that."


"We don't open till noon today." Jake passed some coffee to Darcy, who shook her head. "What's the matter with you? You look terrible."

"I didn't sleep very well." Darcy avoided his eyes and turned her cup slowly on the table. She felt Jake's stare upon her, then felt it shift away.

"Bats?" he asked casually.

She shrugged and took a swallow she really didn't want. "I dreamed someone was in my room." She glanced at his face, but his expression didn't change. "Why aren't you ever home?"

Her question seemed to catch him off-guard. He took a long time washing his hands at the sink . . . drying them on a towel.

"I have a club to run."

"And that takes *all* your time?"

He shrugged. "Most of it, yeah."

"But it closes, doesn't it? And you're never home—" She broke off abruptly, sensing that she'd pushed too far. He put his cup into the sink. A muscle clenched in his jaw.

"Don't nag me, Darcy, I told you I hate that."

"I didn't mean to," she mumbled.

"You sound just like . . . you know . . . and just like Liz—" He stopped, shaking his head, and turned on the hot water.

"Liz said you and she are very close."

"Yeah, she'd like that, wouldn't she?"

"Would she?" Darcy went on innocently. "Have you two gone out or something?"

"Once. When she was trying to get back at Brandon . . . only I didn't know it at the time." He scowled, as if angry for having revealed that much of himself. "I really hate girls like that," he added coldly.

"But you didn't know," Darcy said gently. "Did . . . did that hurt you? When you found out?"

"I hate it," Jake went on, as if he hadn't even heard her. "Girls like that just take and take and nothing's ever enough. They get their kicks from trying to manipulate guys . . . from humiliating them." He stared long and hard out the window. "Your mom's always been like that, too. It's a real power kind of thing." He glanced over with a wry smile. "But then I guess she doesn't have much good to say about me, either."

Darcy avoided his eyes. "She says you're crazy. And irresponsible."

"Yeah, that's right." Jake snorted. "You just never know what I might do. Which doesn't say much for how she feels about *you*, if she's willing to leave you with *me*."

Darcy stared at her coffee, trying to swallow the lump in her throat. Beside her chair Jake stopped and looked down.

"Stay away from me, Darcy. Understand? Just don't get around me at all."

He pressed his lips together and turned away. Darcy waited for him to say more, but he only picked up a dishrag and began wiping furiously at the counter.

"You really do hate women, don't you?" she whispered.

"So what business is it of yours anyway?" he said quietly. He flung down the rag and started for the door, feeling in his pockets for his keys. His other hand froze on the doorknob, and his eyes flashed in her direction as a strange stiff smile slid across his lips.

"I don't like questions, Darcy. Sometimes it's better not to know things."

Darcy stayed in her seat a long time after he'd gone, a low, steady panic building in the back of her mind. *I can't think about this . . . it's too crazy . . . too horrible. . . . I won't think about this—* She hurried upstairs, trying to escape her dark, ugly suspicions, but they followed her, demanding to be acknowledged. *Too many things, Jake . . . too many strange, frightening things I don't understand. . . .*

Darcy picked up her pillow and flung it against the wall, threw herself across her bed, her fists pressed to her temples, forcing all the bad thoughts away—*and it was Jake in my room last night when Brandon and Kyle showed up, Jake leaning over me, his face so close to my neck. . . .* She closed her eyes and lay still, and then she opened them again and slowly turned her head.

There was a piece of paper lying where her pillow had been.

Startled, she reached out and began to read it.

"Darcy," she began, and even before she was finished, her hand began to shake. . . .

It was a short message. And quite clear.

It was written in blood-red lipstick.

YOU ARE MY CHOSEN ONE

# 18

*I'm not going to get upset over this. Someone's just trying to scare me.*

"Yes, we do private parties," Darcy said mechanically, handing the customer a brochure. "Have a good time." *It'd be so easy to get in. . . . Liz worked here . . . Elliott has a key . . . Jake hides an extra one outside . . . that basement window . . .* "No, ma'am, not too scary. No, they don't move or anything, they just stand there." *There's no telling how long that note's been in my room—just because I happened to find it today.* "No, sir, we're not a restaurant, we're more like a horror museum. Sorry."

Gratefully Darcy watched another group disappear into the Dungeon, emptying the lobby. She leaned wearily onto the counter, cradling her head on her arms. She wished she could talk to someone, but the only one here was Elliott. She had no idea where Kyle and Brandon were, but after Liz's little performance last night, she didn't dare call Brandon's house and leave a message. *Maybe he's at rehearsals.* . . . She looked longingly at the door. There was no way she could leave right now, and she wasn't even sure there *were* rehearsals on Sunday. *Chosen one . . . what does that mean?*

"Darcy?"

She jumped as a hand touched her arm, and she found herself looking back at her own face in Elliott's dark glasses. The miniature Darcy looked pale and frightened, and the real one stepped back.

"What do you want, Elliott?" She stared at his glasses and resisted an urge to run upstairs and lock the door.

Elliott's head bowed slightly. A shadow seemed to pass beneath the lenses. "You always stare at me. Like you think I can't see you."

"I . . ." Darcy's hand crept to the pocket of her jeans, where she'd thrust the note. "I don't mean to stare."

Lifting one hand, Elliott slowly drew off his glasses, his pale gray eyes blinking calmly as she took another step back. "Here. I'll take them off."

"No—I mean, you don't have to—"

"It makes some people nervous," he said softly. "When they look in my eyes. It makes some people scared."

To Darcy's relief the phone rang, and she hurried behind the counter to answer it. "Dungeon of Horrors—may I help you?" Then putting one hand across the mouthpiece, she nodded at Elliott.

"Don't you think you should be watching those people going through?"

Elliott hesitated, as though her words were sinking in, then he slipped his glasses back on and slunk out of sight through the beaded curtain. Letting out a deep breath, Darcy went back to her phone call. She was surprised at the deep imprint in her hand when she hung up the receiver. She hadn't realized how tightly she'd been holding it— as if it were her only link with the outside world.

People began filing out, clustering around the counter for souvenirs. Darcy threw herself into hostessing, not wanting to think about the note anymore, but the message had burned itself into her brain. "Yes, I have lots more postcards of the Dracula exhibit. . . ." *You are my chosen one.* "Yes, sir, the guillotine is real—and sharp. . . ." *Jake was in my room last night . . . bending over me . . . watching me sleep. . . .* "I'm not sure about the Space Cannibal—I don't think I've ever heard of that movie."

Darcy's head came up slowly and the room receded around her in a blur. All the events of the past few days began spinning furiously through her mind—doubts . . . fears . . . all forming a terrible pattern . . . a dark, frightening revelation. . . .

"Miss? Miss, are you all right?"

Darcy came back in slow motion. "Yes . . . yes, I'm fine. . . ."

*You are my chosen one.*

*Chosen for what? Death at the hands of a deranged killer? The Vampire's next victim? Then . . . does he know me?*

*Do I know him?*

She was never so glad to see the place clear out. Turning the Closed sign out, she started toward the office when she heard someone tap on the door. Impatiently she inched it open, speaking near the crack. "Sorry, we open again at ten tomorrow."

"Come on, it's just us." A voice laughed, and Darcy threw the door open, flinging herself first into Brandon's arms and then Kyle's, while the boys regarded her in dismay.

"Oh, God, I'm so glad to see you!" She pulled them inside and latched the door behind them. "I really need to talk to you."

"What's up?" Brandon's smile faded, and he caught Darcy's shoulders in a steadying grip as Kyle looked on worriedly. "Hey . . . easy . . . was there trouble here or something? Where's Elliott?"

"No. I don't know." She shook her head in frustration. "I mean, no, there wasn't trouble here, but something happened, and I don't know where Elliott is, I guess he left—"

"Whoa—" Brandon was pushing her gently down into a chair. "Are you hurt or something?"

"I'll call Jake," Kyle began, but Darcy put a restraining hand on his arm.

"No." Again she shook her head, wringing her hands together. "There's just so much I have to tell you."

"It's okay, we've got time." Brandon sat in the chair facing her and put one hand on her knee. "Darcy, come on now, what *is* it?"

"I can't believe I'm even saying this"—she fought back tears—"and I don't *want* to say it—I don't even want to *think* it—" She looked at him helplessly, one tear slipping down her cheek. Kyle hovered at Brandon's shoulder, looking distressed. Brandon's face softened, and his hand caressed Darcy's cheek.

"You can tell us," he encouraged.

"No, I can't. You'll think I'm horrible."

"You can," he coaxed again and brought his face close to hers, his expression worried and sad. "Darcy, what's going on?"

"Oh, Brandon," she whispered. "It's . . . about Jake."

"Jake?" Brandon and Kyle exchanged glances. "What about Jake?"

"I'm afraid he's a . . . I mean . . . do you think he could be a murderer?"

The word came out at last, and she stared down at her hands, feeling heavy and sick. The sudden quiet was like the sea rushing through her head. In the doorway the red beads rustled softly as if someone were standing behind them, listening.

"Jake?" After an endless moment Brandon's voice sounded shocked. He cleared his throat and tried again. "Jake? A murderer? What are you *talking* about—"

"The Vampire," Darcy said miserably. She looked at Kyle for support, but he seemed as stunned as Brandon. "All those girls with their throats cut—I saw the bloody towel—I saw the lipstick—and he followed me at the market—"

Brandon was looking more dazed by the minute. "Towel . . . lipstick."

"And he acted so nervous at the market—you can't tell me you didn't notice that—he kept looking around, like he wanted to leave. You remember, he really didn't even want to go with us—and then that girl was dead—"

"What happened?" Brandon was staring at her like she was crazy. "Did something happen today to set you off on this? Where's Jake now? Is he here?"

"I don't know where he is, that's just the point! Jake's so weird and Elliott's so creepy and—" She was fumbling in her pocket and now she waved the note under his nose. "Here. Read this."

Brandon took the note carefully, as if Darcy's odd behavior might be contagious. Another look passed betwen him and Kyle. "What is it?"

"Brandon—please—just read it, okay?" She watched his face as he mouthed each word silently to himself. "Doesn't it all make sense? He told me not to go in his closet—he caught me in there, and he told me not to do it again—"

"God, Darcy, maybe the guy just wants his privacy. Why were you snooping in his closet anyway?"

"That night we were looking for towels—and it was *your* idea to snoop, not mine!"

"I never said snoop, I only said to—"

"That's when I found the lipstick . . . it fell out of some clothes or something."

"And *that* makes him a murderer?" For the first time Brandon sounded like he was trying not to laugh. Kyle turned away so she couldn't see his face. "Maybe he just had a date, and she asked him to hold it for her!"

"I found a towel in there, too. Full of blood-stains. And someone sneaked in with him one night. Jake was bleeding, and the next day his hand was all bandaged. And whoever was talking in his room sounded really scared.''

"And where were you while all this was going on?''

"I . . . listened from the living room.'' She looked at the floor, feeling two pairs of eyes settle on her. "But I can show you the towel.'' She brightened. "It's right upstairs!''

Brandon looked reluctant. Darcy jumped up and grabbed his arm, pulling him toward the stairs. Kyle shrugged and started after them.

"Come on, Darcy,'' Brandon protested, "do you really think we should be doing this?''

"I know you don't believe me, so I'll *prove* it to you.''

As the boys stood uneasily in Jake's bedroom doorway, Darcy rummaged through the junk in the closet.

"What if he comes back?'' Brandon tried to reason with her. "Jake's always been real good to us, Darcy, we don't want to—''

"It's gone,'' Darcy mumbled.

"What? Are you sure?''

"It was right here on the floor, and now it's not. Why would he move just that towel if he didn't have something to hide?''

"Look a little more. Maybe you'll find the knife he used on all his victims.''

"Scalpel,'' Kyle corrected him. "They're pretty sure it was a scalpel.''

"That's it!'' Brandon said excitedly, turning to Kyle. "All this time we wondered where Jake was— he's been going to medical school to be a doctor!''

Kyle ducked his head, trying not to laugh, and Darcy glared at them.

"Don't make fun of me. Don't you understand what might be happening here?"

"I understand that you're freaking out." Brandon held out his arms and motioned her over. "Come here. Has it ever occurred to you that you're reacting just the way Liz wanted you to?"

"Liz?" Darcy looked surprised. "What does Liz have to do with this?"

"Probably everything. I told you when Liz hates someone, she means business. She probably planted that note just to give you a nervous breakdown. I wouldn't want to give her the satisfaction of telling her it worked."

Darcy stood stiffly, eyes narrowed. "You think— Liz—"

"She worked here, I know she had a key. She could have gotten in anytime she wanted." He regarded her for several seconds, then gave an exaggerated shudder. "Boy, you really had it all figured out there for a minute, didn't you? Poor old Jake—"

"He talks to all those monsters down there," Darcy said stubbornly. "I know he thinks they're real—*especially* Dracula. Doesn't that suggest anything to you guys?" She looked pleading, and Kyle finally nodded.

"Well, yeah, I know it *seems* kind of funny, but—"

"Look," said Brandon, "all I know is Jake's a real private person, and I like him a lot. If he wants to talk to mannequins, that doesn't make him a murderer."

Brandon abruptly turned and went back down-stairs, Darcy and Kyle trailing behind. At the lobby door she threw out her last suspicion.

"And there's Elliott," she said adamantly. "I think maybe he's part of it, too."

Brandon turned and looked down at her, his face screwing up in reproach. "Oh, no, not Elliott-in-the-crowd again." He started to reach for her, but Darcy stepped away.

"I'm sorry I even said anything. I thought you'd at least listen."

"I did listen. And I have to give you credit," he said admiringly. "I mean, you figured this whole thing out all by yourself—"

"Forget it. Just forget it."

"Look, Darcy—" Kyle began.

"I thought you were my friends."

"We are," Brandon said, but Darcy took another step back.

"Just leave, okay? I don't need this right now—"

"Oh, come on, Darcy, you're getting all upset over nothing! You're doing just what Liz *wants* you to do!" Brandon spun around, throwing up his hands in frustration. "Living with a vampire under your own roof. . . ."

"Well"—Kyle glanced away, as if reluctant to say what he was going to say—"I mean . . . I can kind of *see* why you'd jump to conclusions." Brandon shot him a patronizing look, and Kyle stammered, "Well . . . like those bats . . . Jake didn't even seem surprised about them. And he *was* jumpy at the market. I noticed it, too."

"And has it ever occurred to either of you that those bats could have been a warning of some kind? A clue to the Vampire's identity? And there's a door on the fire escape that I'm pretty sure opens into Jake's closet."

There was silence as the three of them looked at one another. Brandon scraped his foot along the floor, almost belligerently.

"So what about Elliott, huh? You're always seeing Elliott everywhere you go—where does *he* fit into all this?"

"Come on, Brandon, let's just drop it," Kyle began, but Brandon brushed him off.

"No, man, I'm really interested. I want to know who she suspects and why. I want to know how she's solved this whole weird mystery."

Darcy's tone was defensive. "Well, how should I know? Maybe *he's* the one who picks out the victims and—"

"They're never together," Brandon cut in. "Have you ever seen Jake and Elliott hanging out together?"

"Yes—the night you and Liz had that fight, they *both* showed up at the same—"

"Oh, come on, Darcy, that's only 'cause I called Jake and needed someone to drive my car!"

Brandon's face went pensive, then unexpectedly he chuckled. "Elliott an accomplice. That's really good. This is the guy who believed that the reason he didn't die in his accident was because he was destined to be some sort of savior."

Even Kyle's mouth twitched at that.

"Saint Elliott," Brandon said solemnly, and both of them snickered. Darcy shot them an exasperated look, and their faces went sober again.

"Children," Darcy grumbled. "Both of you. You're acting like little boys—"

"Not like you, of course"—Brandon was trying to keep a straight face—"who's acting completely sane and rational about all this."

"Goodbye." Darcy gave him a shove. "Just please leave."

"Well, don't you want to have dinner with us?" Brandon looked hurt.

"No, I don't. Get out of here."

Brandon started to say something, took a hard look at her face, then seemed to think better of it. As they went out the door, Kyle hesitated, his face sheepish.

"Darcy, I—"

"Don't *you* believe me, Kyle?" She looked earnestly into his face, saw surprise and embarrassment there.

"I believe . . . that you really believe what you think."

Brandon grinned. "Always the diplomat. Kyle, you should definitely go into politics."

"Thanks a lot, Kyle. That's the most noncommittal answer I've ever heard. Don't tell me—you think it's Liz, too."

"I know Liz," he said. "Don't fall into her traps."

"You're certainly one to talk," Darcy retorted, leaving the rat-incident hanging silently in the air between them. She couldn't help feeling smug as he avoided her eyes and looked pained.

"Okay"—Brandon stuck his head back in the doorway—"tell you what. If you can find the knife Jake used, then we'll believe you."

"They don't think it was a knife," Kyle reminded him with a sigh. "They think it was a scalpel."

"Okay, if you can just find *whatever* weapon he used, then we'll believe you."

"And thank *you,* Brandon, for your support."

She watched them leave, then locked up behind them, leaning her head against the wall, trying to organize her thoughts. *I should never have said anything, I can't believe I did that, I'm so stupid.* Even to herself the whole thing sounded crazy now, crazy Uncle Jake a deranged killer, with Elliott his deranged sidekick, suspected by Darcy, his totally deranged niece. *What was I thinking?* With a groan she sat down and buried her head in her hands. She'd never be able to take back what she'd said . . . she'd never be able to live it down. Even now Brandon and Kyle were probably laughing themselves silly. They'd probably tell Jake— they were *sure* to tell Elliott—and she'd know each time one of them looked at her that they were trying not to laugh, that they were thinking how unbelievably *stupid* she was. Worst of all, they'd tell Liz, and wouldn't *she* think it was great, how easily that dumb Darcy played right into her hands—

"Oh, Darcy, grow up," she moaned.

She stood up and turned around. Elliott was peering at her through the beaded curtain.

With a gasp she jumped back, one hand pressed to her pounding heart. He looked so eerie in the half light, the reflection of the glass, his face ghostly pale, yet tinged with a flickering red.

"How long have you been there?" she demanded. "I thought you'd left a long time ago." *How much did you hear, Elliott? How much do you know . . . ?*

Elliott said nothing, just watched her. Darcy moved slowly to the end of the counter and began stacking brochures into small, neat piles.

"You know, Elliott," she said carefully, and she couldn't believe she was doing this, her words spilling out even as she tried to stop them, "I thought I saw you at the Farmer's Market this morning. It's funny, you know? I just looked up, and there you were in the crowd. Just like that day outside the Club. Just like that time at the café." She heard her voice shaking and realized he had stepped out into the room. "It really is funny," she said again, her laugh weak and forced, "because nobody believes you're ever really there." He was directly across from her now, the counter between them. "*Are* you really there, Elliott?" she whispered.

She felt his eyes even though she couldn't see them, felt their slow careful appraisal in the long silence that followed. She tasted fear and tried to swallow, but it stuck in her throat.

"I'm your savior," Elliott murmured. "I'm your hope."

To Darcy's surprise he started around the counter toward her, and she clumsily backed away.

"Stay away from me, Elliott—I mean it."

"Sooner or later," he said hollowly, "it will happen."

He took another step, and Darcy turned and ran, plunging through the beads, their bloodred shimmering closing off her escape—because there *was* no escape now—

Elliott was right behind her.

"Don't run from me, Darcy!"

Elliott's voice echoed off the dark, damp walls

of the tunnels, and Darcy tried to run faster, but the shadows tricked her, played with her, and all the creatures watched, enjoying her panic as she raced past them, searching for a place to hide. She fell out into the last chamber, and she couldn't see Elliott, couldn't hear Elliott behind her anymore, and *I'm very good at hiding, he had said, good at hiding*. . . .

Darcy spotted the barricade at the far end of the room and clambered over into unfamiliar darkness.

It was a distorted world she found herself in.

From the dim ceiling lights she could make out the alcoves, in their half-finished states of confusion . . . mannequins with maniacal stares, half-clothed, posed expectantly without weapons or victims. A beast in chains clawed at an invisible tormentor . . . a deformed executioner lowered an ax that wasn't there. As Darcy hoisted herself up onto one of the stages, she spotted the perfect hiding place—a tarpaulin-covered grave where two body snatchers grinned down in evil anticipation of their find.

Darcy fell to her knees by the make-believe grave and ripped back the canvas sheeting.

And at first it was just too horrible to believe—too horrible to register or even to recognize—the girl lying there in the sunken floor, hands folded upon her breast, like a lifeless statue, only this girl was real, this girl was—

"Liz," Darcy whispered. "Oh . . . my God—"

And she was so still lying there . . . so strangely, strangely white. . . .

Except for the thin line of blood across her throat.

And the two spots of lipstick on her neck.

# 19

My God, Darcy, I just heard—how is she?"

Through the blur of voices in the emergency room, Darcy recognized Jake. She looked up into his pale face and thought of Liz's even paler one.

"Where were you?" she asked numbly.

"Business." He sat down in an empty chair. "They gave me your message when I got back to the Club."

From other chairs around the waiting area, faces looked back at him—faces that were familiar ones, but had been turned to strangers by shock and disbelief. Darcy shook her head and glanced toward the hallway where Liz's parents were talking to Tony the cop. Kyle looked like he might pass out at any second, and Brandon sat next to him, his hand on Kyle's arm. Elliott slouched in one corner, as if he were merely a part of the worn, faded furniture. Darcy felt a slight pressure on her shoulder and realized that Jake was trying to talk to her.

"Tell me what happened," he said gently.

She stared at him and couldn't answer. She didn't *know* what had happened. She knew that Elliott had come after her . . . that Elliott had chased her . . . yet it was Elliott who had called for an ambulance . . . Elliott who had driven her here to the hospital. . . .

"Darcy, what happened?" Jake asked again. He glanced over at Brandon's face, at Kyle's face, both of them watching him. "What's wrong with you guys?" He sounded almost irritable. "Why won't anyone talk to me?"

From the hallway came the sounds of Liz's mother crying. A policeman closed his notepad and looked grim.

"She was in the grave," Darcy said at last, in a voice that sounded like someone she didn't know.

"Grave?" Jake seemed almost to sense what was coming, and Darcy found herself wondering how he knew.

"In one of the new exhibits. Body snatchers. There was a cover over the grave. I—" She broke off as an officer motioned to Jake. He got up slowly and went over to talk. She kept her eyes on the door that separated them all from Liz, but nobody came out to tell them anything. She stared at it for a long, long time. When she felt Jake slip a cup of coffee into her hand, she wondered how many hours had passed.

"It must have been awful for you," Jake said. "I'm sorry."

She watched him sit in the chair next to her, and

she wished she had the strength to get up and move. She really felt like being alone right now. She glanced despondently around the room and took a sip of coffee, scarcely feeling the scalding liquid down her throat. Elliott was watching her, and she looked away. From the corner of her eye she saw him slide to the edge of his chair, perched there as if uncertain whether or not he was allowed to move. Finally he stood up and stayed where he was, but he was turned in her direction, and she could still feel him watching her. She pushed herself up and swallowed the bitter coffee in one gulp.

"I'll be back," she mumbled, and walked quickly out of the room, down the hall to the bathroom.

Once inside she sagged weakly against the sink and splashed cold water on her face. Her reflection looked almost as deathly as Liz's had, and there were dark wells of hopelessness beneath her eyes. *I can't think . . . I don't know what's going on . . . nothing makes sense. . . .* Her eyes traveled over the bathroom walls and ceiling. *I feel like a fugitive trying to make a break.* She bent in close to the glass and rubbed a paper towel down each side of her face. In the background she saw the bathroom door start to open, then stop and move slowly back into place.

Darcy tensed, her eyes widening at the bathroom reflected behind her. The door hadn't closed all the way . . . there was a tiny crack of light near the doorframe, and as she stared at it, she could swear that the door moved again, ever so slightly.

"Is someone there?" she tried to call, but it echoed silently in her head, only a frightened thought.

*I'm imagining things. Who could be after me in*

*a nice safe hospital where there are people I know right down the hall?*

The door shut softly.

Footsteps disappeared rapidly down the hall.

Weakly Darcy turned around and braced her back against the vanity, her eyes glued to the doorway. No outline of light showed now. Nothing moved. Pressing the towel to her face once more, she held it there and allowed herself several muffled cries. Her knees were shaking and she felt like she'd slide right down onto the floor. *Is everyone totally blind and deaf? Doesn't anyone realize what's happening to me?*

Getting ahold of herself, she inched open the door and peered out.

The hallway was empty.

*For heaven's sake, Darcy, it was probably just someone who wanted to use the bathroom, Liz's mother, maybe, a nurse, some other woman in the emergency room, and they got called back and you are definitely way out of control. . . .*

Sighing heavily, she went back to the waiting room but was intercepted by Kyle at the door.

"Darcy, she's going to be okay, they just told us."

"Oh, Kyle, thank God!" Darcy flung her arms around him and they held each other for a long moment. When she finally pulled away, she saw him wipe clumsily at his eyes.

"Mom and Dad are with her now, and they're sending the rest of us home. We're all going to get something to eat, okay?"

"Yes." She nodded, then laid one hand on his cheek. "Are you sure you're all right?"

"Hey—" He shrugged and gave a strangled

sound that might have been a laugh. "She's a real nightmare, right? But"—his voice softened—"she is my sister."

They hugged again and laughed—genuinely this time—and as Darcy pulled away she saw a nurse motioning to her from the end of the hall. Excusing herself, she started for the nurse's station, passing Liz's parents on their way out, watching them hug Kyle and Brandon and stand talking in a group with the others, looking relieved. She smiled to herself and turned as the nurse touched her arm.

"Darcy Thomas?" The nurse gave a tight, professional smile.

"Yes."

"Your friend Liz wants to talk to you." She crooked her finger, indicating for Darcy to follow, and didn't notice the look of surprise on the girl's face. "I can only give you a minute—you shouldn't be going in at all—but she seems very insistent about this."

Darcy was still too surprised to answer. She kept her eyes on the nurse's stiff back as they passed pale green walls and entered a large room where sleeping patients lay separated by curtains and machinery. Darcy balked and felt her stomach turn at the overpowering smell of mortality.

"She's . . . she's not going to die, is she?" Darcy whispered.

"No, but she's in pretty bad shape. The gash on her head was a lot worse than the one on her neck—she must have put up a pretty good fight." The nurse pointed out the bed and added, "She probably won't make much sense—she's pretty much out of it."

Darcy nodded, swallowing over the lump in her throat. What could Liz possibly want with her now? She had a sudden image of Liz climbing out over the siderails and going for her throat, and she guiltily forced it away.

"Liz?"

She stood there, looking down, knowing she shouldn't be so shaken, now that Liz was going to be all right. The girl didn't stir. Fear washed through Darcy, and she wondered if Liz had suddenly died.

"Liz . . . it's Darcy,'" she mumbled.

Slowly Liz's eyes struggled open. She stared a moment without focus, as if Darcy didn't exist. One hand, attached to a tube, groped above the covers, and Darcy reached out and took it gently in her own.

"Liz . . . did you want to see me? It's Darcy."

This time, finally, her words registered. Awareness lit Liz's pupils, and Darcy felt a slight tremor in the frail hand she held.

"Dar . . ." Liz couldn't get the word out, and her hand moved in frustration. Darcy leaned forward until their faces practically touched.

"Yes, Liz, I'm here. Can I do something for you?"

Liz's fingers worked up over Darcy's hand and tried to squeeze it. "Must . . . tell you," she mumbled.

"What?" Darcy turned her head, putting her ear close to the other girl's lips. "What are you—"

"Must," Liz insisted, "must tell you."

"Yes—I'm listening. . . ."

"He . . . he said . . ." The voice trailed away,

and her eyes closed, blinking open again with a supreme effort. "Too hard . . . so . . . sleepy—"

"Liz, please don't talk. I'll come another time, when you're better—"

*"No!"* The fingers clamped down with unexpected strength, and Darcy winced, surprised. "He . . . said—"

"Who said? Go slow, I'm right here."

"Said . . . warning . . . before . . . grabbed me . . . before . . . hit me . . . before . . ."

Darcy felt shivers go up her spine. "Before he . . . hurt you? *Who,* Liz, who did this?'"

The head moved from side to side. "Couldn't see . . . couldn't recognize."

"Not his face? His voice?"

"No. He . . . hit me . . . choked me. I was . . ." The voice cracked. "I'm sorry, Darcy—"

To Darcy's amazement, tears filled Liz's eyes and ran down her too-white cheeks.

"Oh, Liz, don't . . . don't cry—"

"I did . . . the rat. I've been . . . hateful . . . mean. I just didn't want to . . . lose him."

Darcy stared, the confession numbing her. "Brandon," she murmured.

"I . . . need him, Darcy. No friends. Nobody. He's all . . . all I have. . . ."

"Oh, God, Liz." Darcy lifted the girl's hand gently, rested it against her own cheek. "Oh, Liz, it's all right. . . ."

"I was . . . jealous. Tonight . . . wanted . . . scare you."

Darcy thought the words over carefully. "You were going to do something tonight to scare me. After you left the note."

A blank look of confusion. "No . . . note. . . ."

"You didn't leave the note?" But Darcy could tell by her face that Liz didn't know what she was talking about.

"He came out of nowhere . . . the dark . . . grabbed me . . . told me—"

"What? Told you what?"

"You can't tell." Liz's voice thickened, and her eyes looked wild. "If I say . . . you can't tell. He said . . . if I told the police . . . or anyone . . . he'd kill me. He said . . . he'd know . . . if I did—"

Ice went through Darcy's veins. She was so cold and Liz was so cold, and in that instant she couldn't tell which hand was really her own.

"Please . . . *please* . . . promise. . . ."

"Yes"—Darcy nodded mechanically—"I promise. I won't say a word, not to anyone." She saw Liz shiver and thought how small and harmless she looked now in the hospital bed.

"He . . . bent back my head . . . put something . . . against my throat . . ." Liz took a raspy breath. "Dizzy . . . couldn't breathe . . . blacking out—but I . . . felt it . . . cutting me . . . and him . . . holding me . . . so tight . . . so . . . so *angry*. . . ."

Darcy closed her eyes, trying to block out the images, but she still saw Liz's face, Liz's mouth open in a silent scream—

"He was . . . so careful—and it hurt—and he said . . . he said—"

Darcy's eyes opened. She stared down at Liz, reliving the terror.

"Tell me what he said," she whispered.

"He said . . . 'tonight I choose Darcy.' "

# 20

"Are you all right?" Darcy saw a nurse peering anxiously into her face. They were back out in the hall, but she didn't remember getting there.

"I'm all right," she murmured.

"Do you need to sit down?" the nurse persisted and began steering her toward the people at the door. They were all there in their usual group, waiting for her—Kyle and Brandon—*Liz's Brandon*—Elliott . . . dear Uncle Jake . . .

"I don't need to sit down. I'm really fine."

"Tomorrow she probably won't even remember your being there, so don't be surprised. She was pretty heavily sedated."

*You're wrong. This nightmare will be part of Liz for the rest of her life.*

"There you are." Jake stepped forward to meet her. He slipped an arm around her shoulders. "We wondered where you were."

"Did you see Liz?" Kyle sounded hopeful. "It looked like you came out of that room—did they let you see her?"

They were all staring at her now. Jake's arm tightened.

"Did she talk to you?" he asked casually.

"Of course Liz couldn't talk to her." Brandon gave Jake an impatient look. "They put her out— she couldn't talk even if she wanted to."

Jake was watching her closely. After a long moment he shrugged. "I just wondered, is all. Come on. Let's go home."

She felt stiff and unnatural as he pushed her out to the car. Her knees didn't want to bend. Everyone was staring at her so strangely.

"Where we eating?" Brandon spoke up as they prepared to split up in the parking lot.

"I think we better skip it," Jake said, and Darcy again felt his hold tighten around her.

"Come on—all this excitement, I need to eat." Brandon tried to joke, but nobody laughed.

"We're forgetting what a shock Darcy had," Jake reminded them. "She's the one who found Liz, after all. I think I'd better just get her home."

Darcy glanced wildly at Kyle and Brandon. Elliott stood a little apart, working his hands down into his pockets, saying nothing.

"Well, sure." Kyle shrugged, looking embarrassed. "I mean . . . I'm really sorry . . . we just weren't thinking—"

"She still needs to eat," Brandon argued. "Let us take her, and we'll bring her right home."

"I'd just feel better if she was home with me." Jake pulled her suffocatingly close. "After what happened tonight." He looked away. "I'd just feel better."

"Are the cops through at your place?" Brandon asked, but it was Elliott who nodded.

"They looked everything over. But it didn't happen there. It happened outside."

"Well, I know that's what Liz told them, but they should still search your whole place, shouldn't they?" Brandon said. "She probably wasn't thinking too straight—"

"Give me a break, Brandon, they searched, okay? What do you think—the killer's going to hang around and try for two in the same night?"

"Whoa—" Brandon held up his hands and stepped back. "I'm just hungry, man, not interested in a fight."

"Yeah, well, you're not interested in your girlfriend, either. She nearly got killed tonight, and all you can think about is food." He yanked open the car door and practically pushed Darcy inside. As she huddled on the passenger side, she saw Brandon clench his fists and step forward.

"How do you know what I'm thinking?" His voice raised. "How do you know what I feel? Huh?"

She saw Kyle run up and grab his arm even as Brandon shook him off. "Come on, Brandon," Kyle pleaded, "come on—forget it."

"Have you ever felt anything for *anybody?*" Brandon yelled.

Jake got in and slammed the door. Darcy turned and tried to peer out the window as the car spun away, tried to make them see her and understand, even though she couldn't shout back into the street—*Please don't leave me alone with him, please realize what's happening*—

"Sit down, Darcy," Jake snapped. "Put your seatbelt on."

It was just another trap, and as she hooked the harness around herself, Darcy felt like a cornered animal. She started chewing on her fingernail, afraid that if she didn't, she might start screaming. Beside her Jake was like a spring ready to explode.

*Tonight I choose Darcy.*

She closed her eyes, feeling the car flying down the street, taking corners too fast, squealing through intersections, bouncing over curbs. *Tonight I choose Darcy . . . Darcy. . . .* The car skidded sideways, throwing her into the door. She tasted blood and saw that she'd bitten down on her finger. *He knows me . . . he knows my name . . . and I can't tell anyone or Liz will die. . . .*

And then another thought struck her, and she stiffened slowly, a knot twisting her stomach.

Could it be possible—fantastically possible—that Liz was still trying to scare her? That even now Liz could still be jealous and possessive enough to want to get back at her? And that maybe Liz's attack had been only random and coincidental, and she'd given Darcy the twisted message only to terrify her? Could Liz really be that vindictive?

"Stop the car," Darcy mumbled.

"What?"

"Stop the car. I'm going to be sick."

Jake slammed on the brake and reached across her, shoving open the door. As Darcy stumbled out she managed to make it to the curb and gag a few times before she realized there was nothing in her stomach to come up. And then, without planning to—she began to run. She didn't hear Jake shouting or the horn honking—she didn't hear anything until he tackled her, and they went sprawling down onto the sidewalk, and Jake clamped his hand over her mouth, trying to muffle her screams.

"What's the matter with you? Are you crazy?"

He sounded so angry now, and Darcy felt him shaking her, saw him glancing nervously around the deserted street.

"You picked one hell of a place to go nuts on me, you know that? This is probably the worst part of town! And shut up, will you? Get back in the car—"

"No! I want to stay here!"

"Oh, fine. That's just great!" Jake threw up his hands and looked totally disgusted. "It's a perfect night for staying out, with some maniac running loose. Or wait—I have a better idea. Let's just invite him to join us—that'll save him the trouble of finding you."

"Finding me?" Darcy stared at him. "You said save him the trouble of finding me—"

"Well, why would I say finding *us?*" Jake broke in. "The guy isn't interested in men, or haven't you noticed?"

"I don't want to go—" Darcy broke off before she could add "home with you."

"Well, you have to go," Jake grumbled, hauling her to her feet. "I'm responsible for you, so I'm taking you home. What's the big deal anyway?"

"The big deal? Liz is practically dead, that's a pretty big—"

"Look—what happend tonight was bad, okay?

But it could have happened to any girl out there alone after dark. Liz just happened to be in the wrong place at the wrong time."

"I don't believe that! I don't believe it was an accident!"

Jake's eyes narrowed. "Why not, Darcy?" he asked quietly. "Why wouldn't it be?"

She felt panic rising inside of her and tried to change the subject. "How did he get her inside? There were people around all day."

"The cops think maybe through a basement window—there's one at the side of the building, and you can't see it from the street. There's a storeroom down there I never use anymore. He busted the lock and came upstairs. Nobody would have noticed anything 'cause that new section where he put her is closed off."

"Then . . . why did he use the Dungeon?"

"How the hell should I know! Do I look like a criminologist?" He began to pace angrily back and forth. "The cops think he might have wanted to do something like this for a while. The Dungeon's well-known around here; they think it probably appealed to his sense of the macabre. Once Liz was unconscious, he dumped her in the grave and was probably going to finish her off when he got interrupted—"

"How?"

"By customers—by you—by Elliott—by anything!" Jake grabbed her arm. "Come on, get back in the car."

"I don't want to go back there."

"Look, any vampire with half a brain—and I might remind you that they're very cunning—

wouldn't lurk around where we all expect him to lurk." Jake gave a long-suffering sigh. "Now. Come on. Get in the car."

"What if I don't?"

"What if I carry you?"

His tone convinced her he meant it. Miserably Darcy followed him back to the car and climbed in. When they finally reached home, she stood uncertainly in the middle of the living room while Jake carried sheets and pillows back and forth between his room and the attic.

"There." He stood facing her, hands on hips, his expression grim. "You'll feel safer down here, and I've got everything switched. Is there anything else I can do to make you more comfortable?"

His tone was so thick with sarcasm that Darcy grimaced.

"I'm fine. Thanks."

"So delighted to hear it." After a long searching look he turned on his heel and went upstairs, and Darcy went into the bedroom and shut the door.

She couldn't sleep. Over and over Liz's terrified face drifted into her mind . . . the thin band of blood around her throat . . . her frightened warning. *I've got to tell someone. . . . I can't just pretend nothing's happened and wait to be killed. But what if it's only a trick . . . another lie? Do I spend the rest of my summer being terrified of my own shadow . . . ?*

She slipped out of bed and pressed her ear to the door . . . opened it a crack . . . stepped out into the living room. From the attic she could hear the soft drone of Jake snoring. She curled up on the couch, put the phone in her lap, and dialed

Brandon's number. By the last ring she remembered he was probably still out eating, but he answered just as she was hanging up.

"Brandon? Oh, I'm so glad you're home." She was trying to whisper, holding her hand over the mouthpiece, glancing nervously toward the attic stairs.

"Darcy." He sounded relieved. "Oh . . . hi . . . I thought maybe it was the hospital."

"You did?" His reaction surprised her a little. "Why? Is Liz worse? Are you expecting a call?"

"No . . . I just . . ." He tried to laugh at himself. "Well, what I mean is, you never know. She could get worse. Or . . . the killer could try again."

*No, Brandon, you're wrong, it's not Liz he'll be after this time, it's me, only I can't tell you, because the whole thing might really be true. . . .*

"Darcy?"

"I'm sorry, what?" She snapped back with an effort, Liz's face whirling through her brain.

"I said are you okay? What's up?"

"Liz really loves you," she said so unexpectedly that she stared at the phone in surprise.

"Not as much as Liz loves herself," Brandon retorted. "Where did you get such a dumb idea?"

"She told me. At the hospital. She told me . . . how much she needs you."

"Sure. She probably thinks she's dying. People have all kinds of second thoughts when they're dying."

"Brandon . . . I'm not sure this was an act—"

"If you think I'm going to stop seeing you, you're wrong." His voice changed so suddenly, went so cold, that she frowned. "What else did Liz tell you?"

Darcy hesitated, her grip tightening around the phone. "Nothing, really. . . . Brandon, I'm just trying to be fair—"

"Fair has nothing to do with it. If I want to see you, I'll see you." His voice was hard now . . . stony . . . and after a moment's silence he forced a laugh. "I can do what I want, Darcy. I don't need Liz's permission."

Darcy didn't know whether to feel upset or relieved. "Brandon—"

"Is that why you called? Because of Liz?" His tone changed again, softened now with concern and kindness. "Are you sure there's not something else bothering you? What did you and Liz talk about in there?"

Darcy cast another look toward the stairs. "She just—" Biting her lip, she went on, "Jake's acting awfully strange."

She could imagine him, the look on his face, as his voice came back to her tensely. "What do you mean?"

"He's making me really nervous. On the way home I felt sick and kind of panicked, but he made me get back in the car. He's—I don't know—acting so weird and I'm afraid—"

"You're afraid of Jake?" Brandon cut in. "God, Darcy, you still don't think Jake has anything to do with those murders, do you? With what happened to Liz?"

Darcy made herself into a little ball on the corner of the couch, cupping her hand closer around the phone.

"Brandon, who knows the Dungeon better than Jake does? The lipstick, Brandon, that towel—"

"I can't believe I'm hearing this," Brandon said solemnly. "Come on, Darcy—"

For a split second she felt the walls spinning around her . . . closing in . . . *I'm here alone with a murderer, and no one will believe me. . . .*

"Why would Jake hurt Liz?" Brandon wanted to know. "You know, Darcy, I think Liz must have said something to you at the hospital you're not telling me . . . maybe you'd better tell me what she said."

"I . . ." Darcy stopped, drew a ragged breath. "Why would Jake hurt *anyone?* Look, Brandon, a psychopath doesn't particularly have to have a good reason for what he does, he just *does* it."

"Ssh . . . calm down. Tell me what's really wrong."

Darcy froze. "What do you mean? Why do you say that?"

"Because you sound like you're going to fall apart any second." His voice was grave. "Is there something you're not telling me? Did something happen I don't know about?"

She was nodding, but no sound was coming out. *Yes, oh, yes, I'm going to be next, save me, Brandon, please, before it's too late—*

"Darcy—"

"Please, Brandon, I know it's Jake, I just know it is—I—"

She didn't hear the footsteps coming up behind her . . . didn't see the hand reaching out for the phone.

"Hang up," a voice said.

"What?" Darcy spoke louder. "Brandon, what did you say?"

"Say goodbye. And hang up." The voice spoke again, only it wasn't coming from the receiver, she realized now, it was closer, in the room with her, right beside her—

A hand reached out for the phone.

"Brandon . . ." Darcy whispered slowly, "I really need to go now—"

A finger pressed down on the button, and Brandon's voice clicked off.

Darcy raised her eyes to the figure by the couch.

"I wish you hadn't done that," Jake said.

# 21

Darcy tensed, her eyes on the door, but before she could move, Jake had ahold of her wrists.

"Just sit there," he said. "Just sit right there and don't even think about running." As his eyes bored into her, she trembled and gave a choked cry.

"Are you going to kill me?"

She was actually surprised at how resigned she felt . . . surprised at how calm Jake seemed, towering above her, shaking his head slowly as a look of anger went over his face and then faded.

"I should." He shrugged then. "But maybe I'll wait till later." As he turned away and went into the kitchen, Darcy stared in disbelief. She heard the sounds of coffee being made and after a while he came back with two steaming cups, handing her one.

"So." He sank down at the other end of the

couch and sprawled back, stretching out his long legs. "Maybe you better tell me why you think I'm such a psychopath, huh?"

Darcy stared at him, her face going alternately white, then scarlet. Her hand shook so badly that coffee sloshed out, and she had to set the cup down.

"I . . . I . . ." she stammered, and Jake leaned his head back with a sigh.

"Come on, Darcy, I'd really like to hear this. Just start at the beginning. And whatever you do, don't leave out a *thing*."

As he raised an eyebrow and waited, a sudden surge of indignation replaced her fear, and she reached for the phone.

"I'm calling the police." She tried to sound brave, unsettled by his almost lazy indifference.

"Oh, by all means. I've got friends on the force who'd love to hear this. And call Brandon, too, since he's in on this—and Kyle and Elliott, so they won't feel left out—"

"It's not funny!" Darcy burst out, her hand clamping down on the arm of the couch. "How can you sit there like nothing's happened! When everything is so horrible!"

"What?" Jake said quietly. "Your accusing me of murder? Yeah, I guess that's pretty horrible, all right."

Darcy clammed up and laced her fingers together around one knee. She stared straight ahead, and the silence went on and on.

"So what gave me away?" Jake said at last. "My late hours? My sleazy personality?"

"Stop it," Darcy murmured.

Jake leaned toward her, looked hard into her face. "You're really afraid of me, aren't you, Darcy?" He sounded bewildered. "You really think . . ." He left the sentence unfinished and closed his eyes with a groan. "Damn . . ."

"Please let me go,' she whispered, tears filling her eyes.

"Let you go?" Jake echoed. "Go *where?* Your mother doesn't give a *damn* about you—never did, as far as I can tell. Come on, Darcy, I thought we needed each other."

Now it was Darcy's turn to look stunned. As Jake leaped to his feet and began pacing, she brushed hastily at her tears and ran the back of her hand across her runny nose.

"I mean, look at you," Jake muttered, but more to himself than to her as he walked back and forth across the living room. "You're so pretty—so—so *sweet*—you cleaned up the place—"

"But you hated it when I did that!"

"I never said I hated it! I said I couldn't find anything!'

"Well"—Darcy sniffled—"it was such a mess—"

"*It* was such a mess!" Jake stared at her, somewhat incredulously. "*I* was such a mess! I expected a carbon copy of your mother, and instead I got you! God, if I weren't such an honorable guy!"

Darcy straightened, bewildered. "What are you talking about?"

"And if you weren't so damn innocent!" he sputtered. "I'm trying my hardest not to care about you, and you think I'm a murderer!"

As they stared at each other, Jake suddenly

flushed and looked away, and Darcy's eyes widened in shock.

"You didn't even want me here!"

"Don't tell me what I want," Jake said gruffly. "How was I supposed to know you were going to be so nice? How was I supposed to know I was going to—well—you know—like you so much?"

Darcy's mouth fell open. "You . . . you . . . like me?"

"Well, obviously you haven't gotten that impression, since you've decided I'm trying to kill you." Jake sounded indignant.

"Well . . ." Darcy didn't know what to say. She stared numbly at Jake's back and finally mumbled, "The lipstick . . . the towel . . ."

"What lipstick and towel?"

"In your closet—you told me not to go in there—I thought—"

"Well, *excuse* me for wanting some privacy around here!" Jake turned on her. "I'm not sure what lipstick you're talking about, but if it's the one I picked up off the floor in the lobby the other night, you might as well know now that I'm known to use my pockets as temporary trashcans! Is that a crime?"

"But the towel on the floor—it was all bloody—" She broke off abruptly. She couldn't bring herself to admit that she'd eavesdropped on his strange conversation.

"And I told *you* I hurt myself!" Jake waved his bandaged hand under her nose. "So what? I'm so clever that I dump all the evidence of my crimes in my closet?" Jake scowled. "Not only am I a murderer—I'm a stupid one, too!"

"Well . . ." Darcy looked at him helplessly as he began pacing again.

"Not that I owe you any kind of explanation," Jake said grudgingly, "but a guy jumped me after work, and the fight got pretty nasty." He frowned down at his hand. "Not that I owe you a reason," he muttered again.

Darcy pressed her hands against her eyes. The fierce whirling in her brain was beginning to subside. Jake was still stalking back and forth like a caged animal, and she remembered the first time she saw him and how cute she'd thought he was. . . .

"—or maybe your mother warned you I had a psychopathic personality," he was saying to no one in particular. He thought a moment and shrugged. "Or maybe you heard it from one of my old buddies down in the Dungeon—"

"But you talk to them," Darcy spoke up. "You talk about them like they're *alive*—you talk to them like they're all real—"

"Well, great." Jake nodded vigorously. "Yep, you've got me now—put the cuffs on me and just haul me away—"

"Jake," Darcy broke in, "I'm just trying to—"

"So, I talk to them." He turned to her then, calm, composed. "So I take care of them, make sure they look nice for the public . . . fix them when they need fixing. And they're the ones I talk to. 'Cause they never break confidences, they never turn on me. They never blame me or . . . or . . . condemn me . . . or try to change me. They take me for what I am." His voice faded, and his eyes looked full and sad. "Gus was like that . . . and he loved them so much . . . and these dumb statues, they never leave me, you know? They just''— he swallowed hard and looked away—''never leave me.''

Darcy hardly realized she was off the couch. She lay one hand cautiously on his back and felt him tense. He turned around, his look guarded.

''You know, I watched you last night when you were sleeping, and I was wishing you could always be safe and happy . . . and I thought how it'd been so long since I'd really cared about anything.'' He lowered his head, and his voice was almost a whisper. ''So you'll forgive me, right, if I find this murderer theory of yours a real slap in the face.''

She searched his eyes, the odd mixture of hurt and amusement, and she lifted one hand gently to his cheek. He took it before she could touch him and studied her with that same skeptical expression.

''What are you so afraid of, Darcy?'' he whispered.

And suddenly she was in his arms, her head against his chest, his arms tight around her as she clung to him in confused desperation, as she blurted out the story of Liz at the hospital, terrified to do it, hating herself, but telling him just the same, wanting to feel safe and protected, needing to trust someone—

''I don't want to die,'' she sobbed, and he stroked her hair as if she were a child, his voice soothing, hypnotic, as he reassured her.

''No . . . you won't . . . shh, now . . . shh . . .''

And he tucked her into bed and brought her warm milk, helping her hold the glass, guiding it to her lips—

"Drink it," he coaxed, "it'll help you sleep. Sweet, peaceful sleep. . . ."

"I can't," she said, even as she drank it, even as his hand tilted the cup to her lips. "You'll stay, won't you?"

"Of course I will." And still he held her until finally, *finally*—she began to drop off, her head pillowed against him, her words murmuring over and over as in some strange dream—"Don't leave me . . . please . . ."

And "no," Jake promised, holding her, rocking her into sleep. "I'm here, Darcy . . . I'll watch over you. . . ."

"I didn't know what else to do," she tried to tell him, and again he shushed her, his voice like a strange lullaby.

"Of course you didn't," he said. "Who can you really trust?"

"Please stay . . . please . . ."

"I'll watch over you." Jake smiled. "I'll stay with you."

# 22

It was really the strangest dream.

Ceilings above . . . tilting . . . walls spinning . . . her body floating in the air . . . weightless . . . borne on an invisible current that swept her so easily along through the dark. . . .

Through the deep, peaceful . . . blackest dark. . . .

"Jake," Darcy mumbled, and she tried to open her eyes, but her head felt like a block of stone, and her mind couldn't seem to function. With a groan she forced her eyelids open, then lay there in confusion, thinking she hadn't opened her eyes at all because everything was still so black . . . still so empty. . . .

*I must still be asleep . . . I must still be dreaming. . . .*

In her dream she saw a light . . . far away from her . . . and as she tried to focus in on its hazy glow, it grew larger . . . moving through the darkness softly, noiselessly, like a phantom. It came closer, hypnotizing her with its luminescence, and as she stared in a kind of wonder, it hovered in the air beside her and melted into a human face with an aura of pale silver hair.

"Elliott," she mumbled, "what are you doing in my dream?"

And the face was so close now, sharp lines and angles etched against the backdrop of darkness, and the sunglasses hiding a relentless stare. . . .

"This is no dream," Elliott said.

Reality slammed into her with a terrible force. As her mouth opened to scream, she felt a wad of cloth being stuffed inside, and the next thing she knew, her dull limbs were being pinned behind her and tied together with rope.

"Ssh . . ." Elliott whispered. "You don't want to scream. . . . They'll find you if you scream. . . ."

She was trying to wake up now, trying so hard to climb out of the dream, sluggish with sleep and cold, stark terror. She seemed to be lying on some sort of table in a room she didn't recognize, and as she craned her neck to see, her eyes widened in slow-motion fear.

There were heads . . . heads everywhere . . . and arms—hands—torsos—body parts lined up on shelves, scattered across the floor—clumps of hair—dismembered legs—

Darcy gagged on a silent scream and felt Elliott bending over her.

"They're not real," he said softly. "They can't hurt you."

To her horror she felt his hand upon her head . . . felt it trail softly down the side of her neck.

"Why couldn't you have liked me?" he whispered. "You always ran away."

*Where's Jake?* she screamed at him silently. *Oh, God, what have you done with him, what have you done with Jake?*

"This is the workshop," Elliott went on quietly, as if they were having a leisurely visit. "This is where we take care of Jake's family. I help him do that." Elliott bent closer . . . nodded. "Now I'm helping him take care of you."

For a long horrible moment she stared at him, stared into the cloudy black lenses as the true meaning of what he'd said began to break through at last. *Jake! I was right all along—*

She made a frightened sound, and Elliott leaned slowly across her, working his arms beneath her in an awkward embrace. She felt his cool dry skin against her cheek and fought back a wave of nausea.

"Don't be afraid," Elliott murmured. "I've been with you all along. I'll be with you now."

Darcy's mind somersaulted back to the café, to the Club, to the marketplace—*So it was you, Elliott, and Jake knew it all the time—*

She felt him slide away from her. He went softly across the room and stood at a workbench against the opposite wall. Darcy tried to lift herself to get a better view and saw an assortment of knives, scissors, and tools. Elliott picked up a jar and began spooning something into a glass of liquid.

"Do you believe fate can be changed, Darcy?" He spoke slowly, in that same strange monotone, and every movement was deliberate . . . unhurried. "I think . . . sometimes . . . it *can* be . . . that some of us are given the power to do it."

*What are you going to do to me? Oh, God, Elliott, oh, God—*

"It wasn't your fault," Elliott went on, holding the glass up to the light, watching the contents swirl and dissolve. "You were just in the wrong place at the wrong time." He seemed to be satisfied with the concoction he'd mixed. He glanced at her thoughtfully. "You weren't supposed to wake up. It will be better for you to sleep. Then you won't be afraid." As she made another frightened whimper, his face softened in concern. "It won't be long now. Jake will be here soon."

For a split instant she thought she was going to faint, and her mind seemed to collapse beneath the merciless weight of dark imaginings. She thought of all those helpless victims . . . that girl she'd found in the alley . . . that look of surprised horror on the dead girl's face. *But I'm not going to feel it . . . I'll just go to sleep . . . at least I won't feel the scalpel cutting open my throat . . . at least it'll be easy—there are worse ways to die.*

Tears rolled down her cheeks. Salt mixed with an overpowering taste of fear in the back of her throat. *I didn't want it to be you, Jake, even when I thought it was, I never wanted it to be you. . . .* Again she heard his words in the living room, his confession—". . . *trying my hardest not to care about you. . . ." Oh, Darcy, how could you have been so blind!* She thought of Liz at the hospital and how unthreatened she'd feel now with Darcy out of the way. She thought of Kyle and Brandon, imagining the shock and disbelief on their faces when they found out what had happened to her, and *"I like Jake . . . Jake's all right. . . . Elliott's harmless . . . kind to kids and animals*—Would they realize that Elliott really *had* been following her, working for Jake, that the two of them had been planning the murders, working together from the very beginning—

"I was always kind of different."

Darcy's mind struggled back to the horrible present. Elliott was standing beside the table, holding the glass.

"I didn't want to be, I just was. You might understand. Jake said people forget about you, too. That's why I felt close to you. Because we're alike in a way."

Darcy stared at him beseechingly. *Please, Elliott—please let me go—*

"My mother was always nice to me," Elliott said softly. "But she's dying now." He turned to her, his face sad. "I wish she could stay with me always. I wish she could live forever."

Darcy whimpered again, and Elliott lightly touched her cheek. "Oh . . . oh, Darcy . . . I didn't mean to make you sad. I'm sorry." He looked down at her, his expression almost loving, and then seemed to remember the glass in his hand. "Here. You have to drink this now."

She tried to fight him, to twist her head away, and as he struggled to hold her and pull out the gag, she seized the opportunity to scream.

"No, Darcy, no—don't scream—" Elliott seemed distressed, and for the moment forgot the glass as he tried to stuff the cloth back into her mouth.

"Jake wouldn't want you to scream . . . someone might hear you—"

He crammed the rag between her teeth, then tensed as there was a knock at the door. On the table Darcy froze, her lips moving in a desperate, silent prayer. Elliott patted her reassuringly and moved across the room, looking relieved.

"That's Jake," he said. He put one hand on the door and looked back at her. She heard the click of the lock releasing. "It's time, Darcy," he said. "It's time for it all to be over."

Darcy saw the door swing slowly inward.

And then what happened was a blur.

There was a crash—a cry—and Elliott flew backward into the wall as a figure came hurtling into the room. In the dim light she saw the look on Elliott's face—the total, shocked surprise—and as the other figure pounced on him, they fell and rolled across the floor. As they moved out into a pool of light, Darcy saw the other's face and felt her heart leap.

*Kyle!*

Working at her ropes, she managed to squirm onto her side but couldn't get her body to sit up. She tried to yell, to scream, but only gurgled in frustration. The two boys slammed into the furniture and the walls, severed limbs raining down upon them, glass breaking, instruments clattering around their heads.

Darcy saw Elliott's arm flail up and grope wildly along the workbench—

She saw the gleam of a knife and tried in vain to cry out a warning—

The boys stumbled to their feet, locked together.

Elliott's blade aimed downward. Without warning there was a cry, and Darcy saw Elliott hit the wall, an expression of disbelief draining his face white.

In the terrible silence Darcy stared at him . . . at the slash of red across his stomach . . . the blood soaking through his ripped shirt . . . flowing down his jeans. . . .

Elliott crumpled to the floor. And then, as if released from some awful spell, Kyle finally looked at her.

"Darcy—oh, my God—"

She was crying as he lifted her up in his arms, as he held her close, tears filling his eyes.

"I can't believe it—I thought I'd lost you—" He pressed her tight against him, and as she tried frantically to talk, he pulled the gag from her mouth.

"Oh, Kyle, it was Jake—and Elliott—I was right—all those girls—"

"I know, I know, but you're okay now—"

"But Elliott was waiting for Jake—Jake's coming here! Hurry and untie me—"

Kyle looked toward the door, and her words choked off as he squeezed her up against him. "Shh—I thought I heard something."

As they froze there, not daring to move, Darcy wondered how they would ever escape. She could feel Kyle's fear as he got the ropes off her wrists, and after what seemed like forever, he took a cautious step toward the door.

"Brandon was supposed to be taking care of Jake," he whispered. "I wonder if something went wrong." A flash of panic went across his face, and he grabbed her hand. "Come on—I've got to get you out of here!'

Darcy had no idea where they were or where they were going, but as Kyle led her down a hall and up some stairs, she guessed that they had been in the basement. Now, as Kyle hesitated before another door and pushed it open, she was surprised to see the unfinished section of the Dungeon, with the tunnels winding off ahead of them. Darcy slumped against him, and he steadied her.

"Can you walk?" he asked worriedly.

"I think so . . . Jake drugged me . . . I'll try. . . ."

"Shh," Kyle warned, squeezing her hand. "If something's gone wrong, I don't know where Jake might be. He knows this place better than anyone—he could be anywhere."

Darcy nodded and buried her head against his shoulder. Could something have really gone wrong? Could Jake be stalking them even now? Could something horrible have happened to Brandon? As Kyle guided her carefully along the tunnels, she tried to concentrate on walking, but her legs felt like rubber. The darkness was terrifying to her now—full of noises and shadows that could betray them. *Jake could be anywhere—anywhere!* The life-like creatures stood by and watched them, and she knew they enjoyed her terror, trying to confuse her, hoping she'd get lost. She thought of Elliott and the blood pouring out of his stomach—*It could have been me with blood pouring out of my throat!*

"Hurry," she begged, "please . . ."

She thought she heard something—*a footstep?* Kyle pushed her back against the wall and flattened himself beside her. She felt his quick intake of breath and the tautness of his muscles. From where they

stood hidden, she had a clear view of Dr. Frankenstein's laboratory—the monster, the bottles, the spec-
imens in jars, the trays of bandages and medicines
and gleaming surgical instruments . . .

Darcy's brow furrowed as something tried to
penetrate her senses.

*Gleaming surgical instruments . . .*

Her eyes widened slowly.

The trays of surgical instruments . . . all laid out
so neat so clean, so precise—only there was a
space on the tray that hadn't been there before—
a gap between the shiny silver cutting and stitching
tools where something was obviously missing—

*"If you can just find whatever weapon he used,
then we'll believe you. . . ."* Brandon's challenge
came back to her now, and she leaned closer to
Kyle's ear.

"The scalpel!" She tried to tell him, but her
words were thick and slow. "Jake used the scalpel
on those girls! It was here all the time!"

"The . . . scalpel—" Kyle's eyes were as big as
her own, and he glanced quickly toward the surgical tray.

"Kyle—"

"Shh!"

As he moved away from her, she felt a curious
sensation in her knees. She tried to brace herself
against the wall, but she began to slide down.

"I can't stand up anymore," she mumbled. "I'm
so dizzy . . ."

Kyle scooped her up in his arms and began to
move rapidly through the shadows. To Darcy it
was all a dreamy kaleidoscope, muted shades washing over her in strangely comforting waves. She

allowed herself one brief moment of withdrawal, closing her eyes against the rushing darkness, and when she felt Kyle stop again, she opened her eyes, expecting to be in the lobby.

They were on a shadowy stage.

The Dracula exhibit.

She could feel Kyle's breathing, hard and shallow, his sweat-soaked shirt, his quivering muscles. As she looked at him in confusion, he put a finger to his lips and then gently eased her down onto the floor. He moved to the edge of the alcove and looked anxiously up and down the tunnels.

"What is it?" Darcy mumbled, and she was trying so hard to focus in on his face as he glided like liquid through the shadows . . . as he stopped beside Count Dracula . . . as he unfastened the long, black cape . . .

And swept it gently around his own shoulders.

"Kyle," Darcy murmured, "Kyle . . . what are you—"

And his eyes were so strange when he faced her, glittering like the mannequin's eyes, wide and shiny with a light that didn't look quite real. And he took a step toward her, smiling, as Darcy moved unsteadily away—

"Will you stay with me?" he whispered, moving closer. "You must choose. It must be your choice."

"No—oh, God—Kyle—"

And his hand crept out of the long, black folds of his cape, holding something sharp, something silver and gleaming against the bloodred lining . . .

"Darcy. My chosen one . . . will you stay with me for eternity?"

# 23

It was all so hazy . . . a distorted dream . . . Kyle in slow motion, tying her hands behind her, only he was so quick, so smooth and sure of himself that she never even saw it happen . . . never had time to run. . . .

"They tried to save you," Kyle whispered, knotting the rope so tight that she winced. "They tried to keep you away from me, but they failed, all of them. They should have known better, really. They should—*all*—have known better. . . ." His voice trailed away, and he stood over her, an eerie smile of triumph on his face. "I'm immortal," he murmured. "I'm invincible."

Slowly her head moved—*No, please no*—but his eyes held no compassion, only a frightening kind of power.

"I watched at your window. I put the bats in

that crawl space in your room. I cut the head off the rat . . . and I *enjoyed* it." His expression grew hard. "So who's the *real* actor?" he demanded. "The *true* actor? Who's the best vampire of all?" He stepped away, his eyes traveling lazily over her body. "It was always Liz," he mused. "And I was Liz's brother. And then it was always Brandon . . . and I was Brandon's friend. But I knew . . . deep down . . . I was more than just Kyle . . . I was *someone* . . . someone very different. . . ."

Darcy watched in horrified fascination, his movements commanding yet graceful—as if Dracula's cape had endowed him with a whole different persona.

"When we went to the carnival that night, the gypsy understood. She knew I didn't belong . . . not to *any* world . . . not alive, not dead—just existing. Unhappy. But *she* recognized the power I had inside me. And after she told me, I *knew* I could have my very own world—I didn't need anyone else's."

"Those girls," Darcy said dully. "All those poor girls—"

"I gave them a chance!" Kyle's voice rose defensively. "More of a chance than anyone ever gave me! But—but they didn't understand all I could *give* them—and so . . ." The cape rustled as he shrugged. "I chose for them." He thought a moment, one finger on his lips. His eyes shifted toward her in a sidelong glance. "You're the one I loved, Darcy. You're the one I've *always* loved. You were born for me. You're my chosen bride."

"No . . . Kyle . . . please—"

"Jake and Elliott would have stopped me, you know. They tried to hide you from me—watching you all the time—and I couldn't let *anyone* hurt you.

That's why I had to stop Liz." He smiled a little. "God, how I hate Liz. She doesn't feel anything . . . not like I do. She doesn't care . . . she can't love anyone." His voice hardened, words coming from between clenched teeth. "That red hair and her red mouth and even when she talks, hate—hate—*hate*—red and angry and mean—it *hurts* me. . . ."

Darcy stared at him numbly. "It was *her* lipstick you used. Liz's lipstick on every victim—"

"She deserves to die," Kyle murmured. "She deserves to die over and over again—"

"You're wrong," Darcy whispered. "She doesn't know *how* to love, she *wants* to love—"

"Like she loves Brandon?" His lips curled. "Like she treats him and Jake? Like she treats *me?*" His face grew reflective. "Of course Brandon would want you. But this is one time Brandon doesn't win."

"Kyle—*please don't do this*—"

"It'll be so easy, you'll see. So simple and beautiful, just like a wedding ceremony should be." The scalpel glinted in the half light. "I'm very good. Just a sting, that's all. And then we'll be together. We'll just fall asleep and be together. Always. . . ."

Without warning he swept Darcy up in his arms and carried her across the stage. In a blur of absolute terror she tried to kick and fight, but her limbs were useless and the ropes held her in a merciless grip.

"It won't work—Jake will hear you—he'll be down here any second!"

Kyle stuffed the gag back into her mouth with an apologetic smile.

"I took care of Jake, Darcy. No one will come now. You belong to me."

She saw the open coffin on the floor . . . smooth, satin lining . . . so cool against her skin as Kyle lowered her into it. Darcy struggled to sit up, but he held her firmly on her back, stroking her hair . . . her cheeks . . . her lips . . .

Her throat.

In one graceful movement he climbed in beside her.

Wedged up against him in the narrow space, she felt him work one arm around her shoulders, forcing her head against his chest. And in that position both of his hands met easily behind her back.

"My chosen one," he whispered, "my beautiful bride. Now we'll be as one . . . of the same blood . . . of the same world. . . ."

Frantically she begged him with her eyes. His gaze was full of love and tenderness. She felt his fingers play lightly over one of her bound wrists . . .

She felt the icy sharpness of the scalpel.

"I love you, Darcy," he whispered.

His kiss was gentle.

His hand moved swiftly at her back.

*"Don't do it, Kyle!"* a voice shouted.

With a cry of pain, Darcy felt the slash of the blade on her wrist . . . the warmth oozing down over her hands and arms. As Kyle struggled to close the lid of the coffin, a pair of hands grabbed him and lifted him and flung him out onto the floor.

"You can't destroy me!" Kyle screamed. "And you can't destroy what I *love!*" As Darcy looked on in horror, Kyle clawed at the air, his teeth bared, kicking and biting at the assailant who had wrestled him to the floor.

"Darcy? *Darcy!*"

Someone was yanking at her gag, arms around

her, lifting her up, and *My God, I'm bleeding to
death, help me—*

"Darcy!" Kyle screamed, and his arms were
out, reaching for her, even as someone held him
back. "Darcy, don't let them take me—*we belong
together—Darcy—*"

"Hold him, Jake!" Brandon yelled. "He hurt
her! She's bleeding!"

There was a sickening thud as Kyle's head hit
the floor, and he lay still. Darcy felt her ropes fall
away and heard Brandon swear as he grabbed her
wrists and tossed the gag at Jake. "It's pretty
deep—wrap it up with this! I'll call the police!"

"Elliott . . ." Darcy tried to tell them, but her
voice was so weak, and Jake caught her as she
slumped to the floor. "He got Elliott . . . in the
workroom—"

"I'll go!" Brandon shouted. "Just get her out of
here!"

"Dammit . . . dammit . . ." Jake was all thumbs,
trying to bind up Darcy's hands and keep watch
over Kyle's prone body upon the floor. As he fumbled the makeshift bandage, Darcy suddenly
caught hold of his arm, forcing him to look at her.
For a long time their eyes held . . . and then at
last Jake shook his head. When he spoke, his voice
was trembling.

"Hell of a mess I'd been in, right? Your Aunt
Alicia coming back for you—and you and Dracula
off on your honeymoon—"

Darcy didn't let him finish. She threw her arms
around him as if she'd never let him go.

# 24

**O**f course, you realize," Jake said, scowling, "that all this time you and I were tied for first place as the murderer."

From the hospital bed Elliott gave a wan smile.

"Well, can you blame me?" Darcy chuckled. "Every time I turned around, Elliott was showing up, watching me."

"He was keeping his eye on you a lot more often than you ever knew," Jake retorted. "He's very good at hiding."

"So he told me." Darcy moved closer to the side of the bed, gazing earnestly down into Elliott's face.

"I'm sorry, Elliott. If it hadn't been for you—"

"Come on, let's not get dramatic here," Jake interrupted. "I just didn't trust my creditors, that's all. They've been known to get ugly when they don't get paid." He lifted his bandaged hand and pointed first to the cuts on his face, then to his injured eye, which was finally beginning to resume its normal color. "That's why I had Elliott tailing you in the first place, so they wouldn't get any ideas about using you to get back at me. How was I supposed to know what was really going on?"

"When Jake found out you were staying with him for a while, he told us he was going to put a lookout on you." From the chair in the corner Brandon spoke for the first time. "We didn't think anything about it—we knew Jake owed money to some pretty mean characters. We thought it was a smart thing to do."

Darcy looked at Jake in surprise. "So that's why you told me to stay away from you."

"And why I was so nervous at the market that day—two guys jumped me the night before, and I got some pretty good licks in before they sliced up my hand." Jake shook his head. "Then they tried to burn down the Club. That's when I decided I just can't live like this anymore. So yesterday I went to the cops and to a lawyer to try and get my life back on track. That's where I was when you tried to call me about Liz."

"And you didn't think it was a little strange when all those weird things started happening to me?" Darcy accused them.

"I thought it might be Liz at first," Jake said. "And then I thought you were just imagining things. You know, just coincidences."

"I thought it might be Liz," Brandon admitted.

"Then I thought it might be you," Jake said to Brandon.

"Me! You jerk! Why'd you think it was me?"

"You're too smooth, Brandon—too slick. I've known guys just like you my whole life, and I wouldn't trust any of them." Jake looked like he was trying to hide a smile as Brandon's mouth opened in indignation. "When Darcy told me about Liz's warning, I sat up waiting for you and had Elliott take Darcy and hide her."

"Well, that's just great—"

"You didn't have to drug me, did you?" Darcy joined in.

"I didn't want you getting all nervous," Jake defended himself. "And I'm sorry about the ropes and gag—when I told Elliott to keep you quiet, I didn't know he'd take me so literally! I figured I'd catch Brandon, and you'd sleep through the whole thing. Anyway, if I'd told you I suspected him, you'd never have believed me."

"I don't know . . ." Darcy cast a sly look at Brandon, who was looking injured all over again.

"So Kyle slugged you on the head, and *you* slept through the whole thing," Brandon snorted to Jake. "Some hero."

"Why *did* you come over?" Darcy glanced from Brandon to Jake and back again. "On the phone you thought I was being ridiculous."

"Well, I kept thinking how funny it was, the way you just hung up on me like that, when you'd been so upset. And the more I thought about it, the weirder it seemed. So I finally thought, what the hell, I'll just go over and see for myself if you're okay. That's when I found Jake, and we realized what was really going on. If I hadn't gotten there when I did, I hate to even *think* what would have happened."

The implication was sobering, and their faces went grim.

Elliott's eyes flashed to Darcy, then away. "I found that girl at the market that morning. I touched her, and she was dead. I was scared for you."

Darcy's eyes misted. "Oh, Elliott . . ."

"I thought you would die. I saw it in a dream. That's why I wanted to watch you."

For a long moment there was silence. It was Jake who finally broke it, his voice quiet and uncustomarily sad.

"I never thought about Kyle. He was always the balanced one. The sensitive one. I never dreamed . . ." He trailed off and looked unhappily at Brandon. "How's Liz taking it all?"

Brandon shook his head and looked away. "She said . . . she has a lot of soul-searching to do."

"Yeah, well . . ." Jake mumbled. "Maybe we all do, huh?"

"She wants to see him." Brandon gave a smile. "But Kyle won't do it. I don't know . . . maybe it'll happen. Someday."

Jake straightened, clapping his hands on his thighs, breaking the uncomfortable mood. "So what about you? You and Liz patch things up?"

Brandon shrugged evasively. "Well—hey—us famous actors don't have much time for romance, you know? There's so much adoration out there and so little of us to go around." He looked pleased with himself as Jake laughed. Even Elliott looked amused and shook his head indulgently.

"And anyway"—Brandon cast Jake a sly look—

"I might be pretty busy, visiting Darcy at her aunt's house. She *does* get back tomorrow, right?"

"But you don't know where she lives." Jake stretched and looked totally unperturbed. "I know where she lives . . . but you don't."

"But I can find out—"

"I want *everyone* to come and see me," Darcy broke in, laughing. "I can't stand Aunt . . . Piranha." She winked at Jake, who winked back. "You'll come and get me, won't you, Jake? I mean, I *do* still have a summer job, don't I?"

Brandon raised an eyebrow. "Oh, right. Never trust a guy who lives with monsters, Darcy. He'll either lock you in the attic with his bats or put you in one of his exhibits in the dungeon."

"I've been in one of the exhibits," Darcy returned, deadpan. "I prefer the bats."

"You can tell the future, Elliott." Brandon leaned back, folding his arms lazily across his chest. "Care to give a prediction?"

Elliott looked at Darcy, as if studying her face. "I see happiness," he said quietly. "And people who care about you."

As Jake grinned and Brandon nodded, Darcy reached out to squeeze Elliott's hand.

"Well"—she smiled, nodding at the three who watched her—"*that* would certainly be a nice change."

# About the Author

Richie Tankersley Cusick loves vampires. She reads books and watches movies about them and she is convinced they really exist. Richie enjoys writing when it is rainy and gloomy outside, and likes to have a spooky soundtrack playing in the background. She writes at a desk which originally belonged to a funeral director in the 1800s and which she believes is haunted. Halloween is one of her favorite holidays. She and her husband decorate the entire house, which includes having a body laid out in state in the parlor, lifesize models of Frankenstein's monster, the figure of Death to keep watch, and a scary costume for Hannah, their dog. A neighbor recently told them that a previous owner of the house was feared by all of the neighborhood kids and no one would go to the house on Halloween.

Richie is the author of *The Lifeguard, Trick or Treat, April Fools,* and *Teacher's Pet.* She and her husband, Rick, live outside Kansas City, where she is currently at work on her next novel.